PAGPAG

THE DICTATOR'S AFTERMATH IN THE DIASPORA

BY EILEEN R. TABIOS

FICTION
Behind the Blue Canvas, 2004
Novel Chatelaine, 2009
SILK EGG: Collected Novels 2009-2009, 2011
PAGPAG: The Dictator's Aftermath in the Diaspora, 2020
E (a novella), 2020

POETRY
After the Egyptians Determined The Shape of the World Is A Circle, 1996
Beyond Life Sentences, 1998
The Empty Flagpole (CD with guest artist Mei-mei Berssenbrugge), 2000
Ecstatic Mutations (with short stories and essays), 2001
Reproductions of The Empty Flagpole, 2002
Enheduanna in the 21st Century, 2002
There, Where the Pages Would End, 2003
Menage a Trois With the 21st Century, 2004
Crucial Bliss Epilogues, 2004
The Estrus Gaze(s), 2005
Songs of the Colon, 2005
Post Bling Bling, 2005
I Take Thee, English, For My Beloved, 2005
The Secret Lives of Punctuations, Vol. I, 2006
Dredging for Atlantis, 2006
It's Curtains, 2006
SILENCES: The Autobiography of Loss, 2007
The Singer and Others: Flamenco Hay(na)ku, 2007
The Light Sang As It Left Your Eyes: Our Autobiography, 2007
Nota Bene Eiswein, 2009
Footnotes to Algebra: Uncollected Poems 1995-2009, 2009
On A Pyre: An Ars Poetica, 2010
Roman Holiday, 2010
Hay(na)ku for Haiti, 2010
THE THORN ROSARY: Selected Prose Poems and New 1998-2010, 2010
the relational elations of ORPHANED ALGEBRA (with j/j hastain), 2012
5 Shades of Gray, 2012
THE AWAKENING: A Long Poem Triptych & A Poetics Fragment, 2013
147 Million Orphans (MMXI-MML), 2014
44 RESURRECTIONS, 2014
SUN STIGMATA (Sculpture Poems), 2014
I Forgot Light Burns, 2015
Duende in the Alleys, 2015
INVENT(ST)ORY: Selected Catalog Poems & New (1996-2015), 2015

The Connoisseur of Alleys, 2016
The Gilded Age of Kickstarters, 2016
Excavating the Filipino in Me, 2016
I Forgot Ars Poetica, 2016
AMNESIA: Somebody's Memoir, 2016
THE OPPOSITE OF CLAUSTROPHOBIA: Prime's Anti-Autobiography, 2017
Post-Ecstasy Mutations, 2017
On Green Lawn, The Scent of White, 2017
To Be An Empire Is To Burn, 2017
If They Hadn't Worn White Hoods … (with John Bloomberg-Rissman), 2017
What Shivering Monks Comprehend, 2017
YOUR FATHER IS BALD: Selected Hay(na)ku Poems, 2017
IMMIGRANT: Hay(na)ku & Other Poems In A New Land, 2017
Comprehending Mortality (with John Bloomberg-Rissman), 2017
Big City Cante Intermedio, 2017
WINTER ON WALL STREET: A Novella-in-Verse, 2017
Making National Poetry Month Great Again, 2017
MANHATTAN: An Archaeology, 2017
Love In A Time of Belligerence, 2017
MURDER DEATH RESURRECTION: A Poetry Generator, 2018
TANKA, Vol. I, 2018
HIRAETH: Tercets From The Last Archipelago, 2018
One, Two, Three: Selected Hay(na)ku Poems (Trans. Rebeka Lembo), 2018
THE GREAT AMERICAN NOVEL: Selected Visual Poetry 2001-2019, 2019
The In(ter)vention of the Hay(na)ku: Selected Tercets 1996-2019, 2019
Witness in the Convex Mirror, 2019
Evocare: Collected Tankas (with Ayo Gutierrez and Brian Cain Aene), 2019
WE ARE IT, 2020
Double Take, 2020
Because I Love You, I Become War, 2020

PROSE COLLECTIONS
Black Lightning: Poetry-In-Progress (poetry essays/interviews), 1998
My Romance (art essays with poems), 2002
The Blind Chatelaine's Keys (biography with haybun), 2008
AGAINST MISANTHROPY: A Life in Poetry (2015-1995), 2015
#EileenWritesNovel, 2017

PAGPAG

The Dictator's Aftermath in the Diaspora

Eileen R. Tabios

Paloma Press, 2020

ISBN 978-1-7323025-4-9

Library of Congress Control Number: 2020930702

ALSO FROM PALOMA PRESS:

Blue by Wesley St. Jo & Remé Grefalda
Manhattan: An Archaeology by Eileen R. Tabios
Anne with an E & Me by Wesley St. Jo
Humors by Joel Chace
My Beauty is an Occupiable Space by Anne Gorrick & John Bloomberg-Rissman
peminology by Melinda Luisa de Jesús
Close Apart by Robert Cowan
One, Two, Three: Selected Hay(na)ku Poems by Eileen R. Tabios, translated into Spanish by Rebeka Lembo (Bilingual Edition)
HUMANITY, anthology edited by Eileen R. Tabios
The Great American Novel by Eileen R. Tabios
The Good Mother of Marseille by Christopher X. Shade
Diaspora Volume L by Ivy Alvarez
Elsewhen by Robert Cowan, illustrated by Ada Cowan
Glimpses: A Poetic Memoir by Leny Mendoza Strobel
Shield the Joyous by Christopher X. Shade

PALOMA PRESS
San Mateo & Morgan Hill, California
Publishing Poetry+Prose since 2016
www.palomapress.net

*"The glory of saving a country is not
for him who has contributed to its ruin."*
— José Rizal

from **"When I Was"**

When I was 1

Mama dressed me
in ruffled panties
Each ruffle presented
a different color

Whenever I flipped
(or flopped) over
to show my butt
I revealed a rainbow

When I was 5

I made small books
by folding pieces
of paper. I shelved
them in bookcases
formed from Mama's
shoeboxes. My favorite
bookshelf was red—

a glossy vivid red
whose appearance
never failed to announce
its presence, and mine

When I was 8

An assassin failed
to kill my father

But an assassin did
try to kill my father

The assassin is another
father to my diaspora

When I was 9

I played the piano
in my first and only recital

But the diaspora loomed
All I remember today

are my dress and shoes
both white as ivory piano keys

In the diaspora, even music
can be as dirty as a refugee

When I was 10

I left my birthland—

a wound impossible to heal

When I was 11

I was lonely

When I was 12

I was lonely

When I was 13

I was lonely

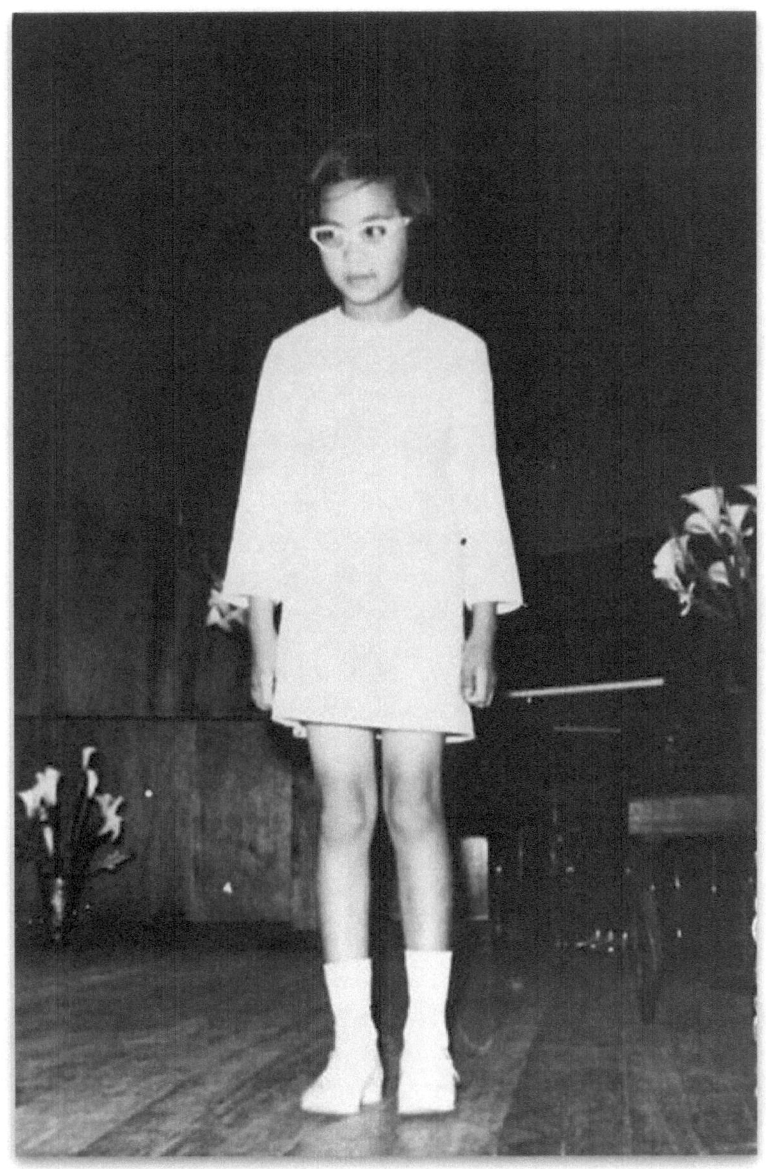

Eileen R. Tabios as an eight- or nine-year-old at her first and last piano recital at St. Louis Elementary School, Baguio City, Philippines

CONTENTS

Introduction

I've been offended for years…for decades. I've been offended at how I came to join the Philippine diaspora. I empathized with my mother in not wanting to leave our birthland. But we did immigrate in 1970 to the United States to join my father who'd left permanently two years earlier. No doubt my parents had hopes of better opportunities. But just days before my father left, an assassin had tried, though failed, to take his life—a sign of the difficulty of being an honest businessman in a land then on the brink of being eaten by the martial law dictatorship of Ferdinand Marcos.

When I started as a creative writer in my mid-thirties, I began with short stories addressing the Philippines. "A Ghost Haunting" (1995) is my first published short story. The story reflects my inexperience as a writer. But I include it because it reflects how the politics of my past has been a haunting. The Philippines is, among other things, a tribal society and there are advantages to my family being Ilokano like Marcos. But it's not hard to transcend tribalism for critique when one knows the damage inflicted by Marcos' martial law. I can remember when many people actually welcomed martial law for such was the lawlessness of the times. How swiftly did that move degrade to years then decades of abusing the powerless. As a political science major at Barnard College, I had written a thesis on the Philippines where I then noted the difficulty of overcoming the conflict of interest that exists when the economic elite is the political elite and politicians are supposed to be in charge of uplifting others besides themselves and their allies. The worry in that old college thesis is affirmed starkly today by the gap between the rich and the poor—according to *The Spectator Index*, there exists 17 billionaires in the Philippines, the same country where "pagpag" is normalized.

Pagpag is the practice of scavenging through trash heaps for discarded food that the poor then attempt to clean and re-cook for new meals. To be clichéd yet sincere, *my heart breaks* at how the poor are forced into this practice…to the extent that it's become normalized (small businesses have cropped up to create and sell pagpag). But it's not okay. Pagpag is never okay—especially in a land where others spend "15 million pesos on a handbag," as noted by novelist-activist Ninotchka Rosca. A serving of pagpag can cost as little as 20 pesos hard-earned by the poor (YouTube features several videos on pagpag, including this from the BBC: https://www.youtube.com/watch?v=c7gDBVmgIRA) For me, pagpag heart-wrenchingly symbolizes like no other the effects of a corrupt government unable to take care of—indeed, abusing—its people.

After writing this set of short stories—most were first published in journals from 1995-2000—I set them aside. Eighteen years later, I returned my attention to them in 2019 (adding the most recent story "On Imitating a Rhinoceros" to create this collection) because the cruelty of Rodrigo Duterte's regime in the Philippines deserves to be protested. Strongman

Duterte is also a logical effect of Marcos' dictatorship which had significantly damaged the future of a young country still coming into its own. I protest, too, Duterte's help in rehabilitating the reputation of the Marcos family, who continue to enjoy the privilege funded by Marcos' thievery of the country's resources to limit the potential of its people. I protest, in part, through this short story collection entitled *PAGPAG*.

While none of my stories directly address pagpag, I think of their tales as among what lurks within the pagpag stew created by a dictator's actions. The aftermath is not always obvious like the imprisoned, the tortured, or the salvaged (murdered); the aftermath goes deep to affect even future generations in a diaspora facilitated by corruption, incompetence, and venality. It certainly seems time, too, to share stories from the point of view of those who left the Philippines as children because their parents had to leave—children who grew up watching and listening to the adults remember the homeland they left behind and who, as adults, can more fully articulate the effect of their histories.

Any country, any society, should be judged by how it treats its most fragile, including its most poor. For a government to tolerate not just the existence but the growth of pagpag activity is to reveal a fundamentally cruel government. I protest.

A writer writes, and here I write in protest—I know writing by itself is not adequate, even as I humbly offer this collection to readers. But I do believe in the ultimate power of the written word and this book would be among those I'd send back from the diaspora to the Philippines through this poem:

ALAALA: A Balikbayan Box for the Residents of Malacanang Palace

A balikbayan box (literally "repatriate box") is a box containing items sent by overseas Filipinos back to the Philippines
      —Wikipedia

—a cardboard box containing Honor
—an envelope containing Humility
—a glass jar containing Accountability
—a plastic bag (made from recycled plastic) containing Compassion
—a wallet containing Ethics

—a can containing a million Apologies for you to make to the Filipino people
—a miniature barrel ~~containing~~ reversing the Diaspora

—a shopping bag stuffed with Iranian rials

—a faux Limoges trinket box containing Memory
—a bento box containing the histories of Spain, England, France,
Netherlands, Portugal, and the United States

—a Manila envelope bulging with the poems of Joi Barrios

—DVDs presenting Nick DeOcampo's directed "Revolutions
Happen Like Refrains in a Song"
    Kidlat Tahimik's "Why Is Yellow the Middle of the Rainbow?"
    Kara Magsanoc-Alikpala's "Batas Militar"
    Ramona Diaz's "Imelda"
    Kara David's "1081"
    Ed Lingao's "Lest We Forget: Martial Law and its Victims"
    Sari Lluch Dalena and Kiri Lluch Dalena's "The Guerilla Is a
    Poet"
    J Luis Burgos' "Portraits of Mosquito Press"
    Sari Lluch Dalena's "Dahling Nick"
    Teng Mangansakan's "Forbidden Memory"
    Adolfo Alix Jr.'s "Alaala"
    Sari Lluch Dalena and Keith Sicat's "History of the
    Underground"

—a pair of boxing gloves left by a Manong who worked Hawai'i's
sugarcane fields
—a dull knife left by a Manong who worked in Alaska's fish
canneries
—a handkerchief left by my grandfather, a Manong I never knew

—a tree limb from Clody Cates and Gaige Qualmann who created
tree limbs from harvested illegal weapons in San Francisco
—a thousand jewelry boxes with earrings crafted from bullets
melted by an anonymous Cambodian artist

—a____
[Second-Generation Reader, fill in the blank]

—books
—books
—books
—Books

—Eileen R. Tabios
Saint Helena, California, the indigenous land of the Wappo
January 1, 2020

Collected Protest Stories 1995-2001 Plus One

Negros

"Daaaaaa — deeeeeeee! Daddy, Daaaaaa — deeeeeeee!"

My mother did not look dignified yelling down the mountain. Her hands flapped like the wings of chickens we chased for dinner, her blouse escaped from the waistband of her skirt, her hair streamed in all directions from her loosened bun and her mouth thinned around a circle of prominent teeth. She screeched from the balcony of our house which stood on top of Mount Asawa. She, most assuredly, would have been dismayed if she realized that her voice topped that of Auntie Feling's whose water broke when she was visiting the previous month. Clutching her belly, Auntie Feling's exhortations to call the doctor had been audible even to the traffic on the road circling the bottom of the mountain.

Mount Asawa was actually a hill, but everyone was accustomed to calling it a mountain because of its name. The other thing about its name was that "Asawa" could mean "wife" in Tagalog. Thus, my father's friends always enjoyed a rollicking good time discussing the many ways to "Mount Wife."

Anyway, there was my father's asawa ordering me and my father as we were half-way up the mountain to hurry in a voice loud enough to carry to Manila. We broke into a run, wondering what disaster had befallen the household. My father had gained weight over the years but he easily ran ahead of me—his quivering backside, encased tightly in brown polyester, looked like the rump of a well-fed carabao.

As we burst into the house, the servants were running through the living room, much like the time Mama stood barefoot on the sofa and screamed at the unexpected visit of a neighbor's pet monkey who slipped in through an open window, "Ayyyyyyyy-susssss! Everyone get that lice-ridden creature before he tracks his diseases through the house!"

This time, my mother was instructing all the servants, "Black, black, as much black as you can find!" before dashing off toward the servants' quarters.

"What's going on here?" my father demanded as we followed my mother. We entered Manang Inday's bedroom where we found the maid lying on her bed, clutching her knees to her chest, mumbling and shivering despite the heat.

"Ayyyyy-susssss!" We finally deciphered some of Manang Inday's mutterings. "I am freezing!"

My mother started layering the clothes bundled in her arms over Manang Inday as my father and I watched, open-mouthed with amazement. I reached for my father's hand which returned my clasp firmly.

"Her body has been taken over by a mamau," Mama explained, her perspiring face looking back at us and inviting us to share in the horror of the matter.

"Mamau—a ghost?" I repeated, concerned and moving behind my father. My father closed the cavern of his mouth and snorted.

"Another ghost? Why did we move to this place," my father complained, releasing my hand as he disgustedly flung both of his up in the air. "Ever since we arrived in this city, I've been haunted by floods, neighbors who eat the evidence of their depletion of my chickens, a roof that won't stop leaking and a different ghost showing its pathetic presence every month! Are these mamaus breeding behind the chicken coop?"

Then my father laughed at the ceiling, apparently thinking he inadvertently displayed some wit. I smirked, too, as his lack of fear made me unafraid.

"Well, and what does this ghost want this time," my father asked after he stopped barking to himself at the sight of Mama's frown.

"Have you no respect? The body of Inday, who could never hurt a soul and, undoubtedly, was just minding her own business, has just been invaded by an unwelcome visitor from the other realm!" my mother, her hands on her hips, chastised my father.

"The other realm?" my father mocked, his voice a sudden squeak. As the warning look became murderous on Mama's face, he calmed himself, smoothing back the sparse strands over his glistening scalp. He sat in the lone chair of the room which, next to the servant's bed, allowed for a direct look into Manang Inday's grimacing face. He pulled me to his side and whispered, "We're in this together, buddy. Let's discover the surprise *du jour*!"

Du jour was French and meant "of the day." My father loved to teach pieces of trivia that he thought I would not learn otherwise from the nuns at my elementary school.

"Alright, let's hear it," my father said, sinking his chin into his chest with the demeanor of preparing for a long, tedious story. His profile was that of a multi-bellied Buddha in a yellow, short-sleeved golf shirt. "But first, why did you cover Inday with your slips? Isn't it better to cover her with a blanket than your underwear?"

My mother dropped her eyes and blushed before she responded, "My slips are black. Nana Sitang said that if ever a ghost takes over the body of someone in our household, we should cover the body with black material because black feels more comfortable to a mamau."

I remembered Nana Sitang's visit to our home and the conversation turning to the nature of ghosts. But Nana Sitang could not explain why black was more comfortable to mamaus or why the comfort of ghosts was significant, only that she had managed to pick up these gems of wisdom from her village's witch doctor when she was a teenager. Of course, she had cackled through tobacco-stained teeth, this was before Nana Sitang's parents discovered and put a stop to her visits to the witch doctor who also dabbled as the bookie at local cockfights. Before my father could remind Mama of these points, we heard a slight scuffling noise behind us.

"Oh, good, Neta, you found more black," my mother said to one of the servants who stood just beyond the doorway, her head tilted away from looking into the room as if there was a disease she could catch by just looking. Manang Neta blindly held out a bundle of clothes. Sighing, Mama allowed Manang Neta to avoid entering the room and went over to take the pile from her hands.

"Hey, that's my jacket," I piped up as I noticed one of the articles of clothing my mother was layering over Manang Inday from the results of Manang Neta's forage through the closets.

"Shussssh, boy," my father ordered. "Why do you need a jacket when you live in a tropical country?"

"But it's American and from Uncle Cosmo," I mumbled to myself, ignoring his lesson that I lived in a "tropical country" and wishing only to retrieve the jacket my favorite uncle had sent me for my tenth birthday. My jacket was black with a picture of Captain Kirk, Mr. Spock and Dr. McCoy on the back.

"Okay, Gloria, what does *this* ghost want?" I could tell my father was losing patience by the way he emphasized his words. Since we moved from Manila to Baguio City three months ago, we had been visited by three ghosts, including the one who inhabited Manang Inday's body.

The first was a dark shadow that hovered outside my parents' bedroom window and pleaded for any old clothes that they could spare. The ghost made its request in what my father called "a whining, toadying tone that no self-respecting ghost would ever use because real ghosts should have no reason to behave towards humans in a servile manner!" In disgust, my father threw out his old bathrobe but refused to let my frightened mother empty the drawers for more clothes to dispense out the window.

"It's only a loko-loko from the neighborhood trying to stiff us," he said, waving at her to return to bed and slamming the shutters closed. However, since my parents' bedroom overlooked the air over a steep-sided valley created by one side of Mount Asawa, we have never determined how a person could have managed to throw a shadow from right beyond my parents' bedroom window.

The second ghost appeared a month later and took the shape of my father's old bathrobe floating beyond the bathroom window when my mother had to exercise an act of nature in the middle of the night. With one frayed sleeve pointing at my mother, the mamau chastised my parents for their selfishness. The tunnel-like darkness of the empty sleeve reminded her, my mother later said, of the throat of a shark who had opened its jaws at her when she was a little girl swimming in the seashore by the fishing village where she was born. My mother decided to make a generous donation to the local orphanage the following day, much to my father's dismay.

"You weren't there!" Mama replied heatedly over breakfast after my father berated her for confusing dreams with reality. I sneaked a forgotten mango slice from my mother's plate as I waited for my father's response.

"Of course I wasn't there! Since when have I ever accompanied you to do your Number 2? It does not smell sweet, madam!" my father roared back, stabbing his fork in the air and breaching one of my mother's rules of never pointing an eating utensil towards the direction of another. But my father's anger did not accomplish anything as my mother proceeded later that day with her gift to the orphanage.

"*Susmaryosep*! Don't use that tone of voice with me," Mama snapped back at my father as they discussed the third ghost. "You can listen, too, with your elephant-sized ears as I question the spirit."

By expressing "Susmaryosep" instead of the shortcut, "Ayyyyy-sussss," I could tell my mother was really agitated. "Susmaryosep" is short for "Jesus, Mary, Joseph" whose names my relatives frequently invoked in moments of stress.

My mother bent over Manang Inday's quivering face. Poor Manang Inday, I thought as I always did whenever I happened to pay attention to her. Her face bore a distinct resemblance to Uncle Fillmore's bulldog: the same mournful brown eyes surrounded by drooping lids; the slack, multi-layered folds below the chin; and a bulbuous forehead. Uncle Fillmore had noticed the resemblance upon acquiring the bulldog, and so named it after Manang Inday, much to the distress of his wife, my Auntie Feling who surely must have busted one of Uncle Fillmore's eardrums with her views on the matter.

"Now, now. You should be warmer now," Mama crooned, her face about an inch away from the bump protruding from the tip of Manang Inday's nose. "Who are you and why are you visiting us through poor Inday's body?"

Manang Inday started to act like a fish, disconcerting my mother and causing her to move closer to us. The servant's lips kept shifting as she breathed through her mouth. Finally, the ghost discovered that one can breathe more easily through a nose and, after a few times of becoming accustomed to this notion, used Manang Inday's mouth for speaking.

"Is that you, my little garbage can?" Manang Inday, or rather, the mamau, asked. It had to be the ghost because the voice did not sound like Manang Inday's voice. The voice was melodious instead of Manang Inday's which has reminded many listeners of the braying of a constipated goat.

"Is that you, my little garbage can?" the ghost repeated lovingly.

"Yes," Mama could manage only one word through the surprise, then the prolonged wince contorting her features.

"Mama, why is she calling you a garbage can?" I asked the question, as well on behalf of my father as, both wide-eyed, we looked at her.

The mamau laughed with Manang Inday's face: soft rolling peals that sounded like the hymn being outlined on air whenever the bells tolled from the church another hilltop away.

"My little garbage can, this must be your son, Matthew," the ghost said. "Well, I'll tell you why, my sweet boy."

I scowled at being called "sweet" but leaned closer with my parents toward Manang Inday's body. The mamau's voice was full of mischief, courting us with the manner of sharing confidences.

"When your mother was a little baby, I helped take care of her. We would spend many afternoons in the shade of the biggest star apple tree in your grandmother's yard. There we would sit, I rocking her back and forth while I feasted on my little bags of sweets.

"Oooohhhh, I had such a sweet tooth," the ghost said with an air of self-congratulation. "I always carried around bags of churros, susporos de casuys, palitaos, polvarons, maja blancas, maruyas and bibingka. My favorite was puto maya; I loved to watch my mother make it with sweet rice, coconut milk, brown sugar and grated coconut meat. My, my, they were so delicious!"

Here, the mamau interrupted herself with a few choice smacks of Manang Inday's lips. My mouth also started to water.

"One day, your mother started crying and crying. I kept rocking her and patting her on the back but she wouldn't stop bawling. Then I noticed her small chubby hands reaching into my bag of sweets. Your Mama wanted some, too.

"Well, she was just a baby and couldn't have eaten the snacks with her soft, little gums. So, after much thought, I chewed and chewed a tiny piece of my favorite *puto maya* and then fed the result to her. She loved that so much. And that's how she became my garbage can. Because I would chew sweets and feed them to her, directly from my mouth with a kiss."

"Eeeeeeuuuuuuuwwwwwwwhhhhhh," my father cried out before we both burst in laughter and pointed our fingers at my mother who was standing still with a pained look on her face. Mama tried to hide her embarrassment by starting to straighten her blouse and smooth her hair back into her bun.

"That's why you're a garbage can, because you ate her leftovers when you were a baby?" I wheezed between my laughter.

"Aaahhh, but Matthew, she was *my* little garbage can and I so loved my honey honey bun bun," the ghost noted, screwing up Manang Inday's lips into a grin wide enough to display the blackened fillings in all of Manang Inday's cavities.

My father elbowed me to look at him. Cross-eyed, he started whispering in a sing-song, "honey honey bun bun." Choking on my laughter, I bent over and crossed my legs as I felt my bladder begin to expand.

My mother cleared her throat and asked in as business-like a demeanor as she could manage, "Auntie Lina, why are you here? What can we do for you?"

"I'll tell you, my darling, but before I do could you please bring me something hot to drink? I am so co o o o ld," the ghost replied and made Manang Inday's body shiver exaggeratedly.

Mama quickly called for Manang Neta. Manang Neta showed the back of her uncombed head again since she still refused to look into the room. "Yes, Ma'am?" she squeaked.

"Heat up some Campbell's," Mama instructed.

"Yes, Ma'am," Manang Neta squeaked again and ran away to the kitchen.

"Campbell's soup? How kind of you to share such luxuries as American food," the ghost said gratefully.

"But now, let me tell you why I'm here. Do you remember, my little garbage can, your distant cousin, Eliel?"

"Only vaguely, Auntie Lina. Doesn't he now live in Negros?" Mama asked, referring to Negros Occidental, the country's primary sugar-growing province.

"Yes, yes. Things are bad in Negros for your cousin's family. My heart breaks to see Eliel so skinny. He refuses to eat because his children do not receive full sustenance from the little that he can offer them. Yet he's the one who must remain strong to be able to harvest the sugarcane and do any other work required to feed his family," the ghost nodded Manang Inday's face up and down as she sighed.

"That is sad," Mama said. Solemnly, my father and I nodded our heads in agreement.

"Well, you and Andrew are doing so well here in Baguio City, two well-educated professionals that you are," the ghost continued. "Congratulations, Andrew, on your recent promotion to Senior Vice President at Banco Baguio! My goodness—you've become such a big-shot banker! And, Gloria, to be principal of Baguio High School—what a coup!"

"You don't have to explain, Auntie Lina. We will be more than happy to help," my mother quickly interrupted. Mama later told me that hearing the *mamau* recite our family's good fortunes made her uneasy. "Never take blessings for granted, Matthew," my mother warned.

Unlike with the other two ghosts, my father did not utter a single word of complaint over my mother's offer to provide assistance. Sighing, he only pulled me closer and looked sadly at my mother.

After my mother agreed to help Uncle Eliel, the mamau did not speak again, despite my mother's questions and other attempts to engage her in conversation. She only indicated her presence by intermittently making Manang Inday's body relapse into a fit of shivers until Manang Neta brought the soup. The ghost still uttered no words as she finished a bowl of Campbell's noodles in chicken broth. After she emptied the bowl and emitted a loud burp, Manang Inday's body sat up on the bed with a startled look on her face, the layered clothes flung off in a disarray around her. When Manang Inday brayed at us familiarly like a goat, then we knew the ghost had departed.

❧

Before we immigrated to the United States three years later, Uncle Fillmore and Auntie Feling agreed to my father's request that they take over providing assistance to Uncle Eliel and his family. After the third ghost's visit, Mama dispatched a servant with packages of food and money every six months to travel the hundreds of miles to Negros which was located on the southern part of the Philippine archipelago.

As I helped my mother the day after the incident to pack the first set of provisions to Negros, Mama mentioned that she doubted the mamau was actually Auntie Lina because she inhaled and drank the soup so loudly.

"Your Auntie Lina never would have slurped. She was a lady," my mother emphasized, her hands patting at the bun on her head to ensure that it had trapped all the stray strands of her hair.

"Yes, Mama," I agreed dutifully, and then asked, "But Mama, why did you consent to helping Uncle Eliel if you didn't believe that the ghost was Auntie Lina?"

"Because Negros is Negros, my son. And I had no doubt Eliel's family needed help. The ghost was just reminding me, that's all," Mama replied before turning aside and bending down to look at something in the rug.

She would have been upset if she knew I saw the teardrop sliding down her nose, I thought as I allowed her to pretend to rub away at an invisible stain on the rug.

Later, as we were packing to leave the country, my mother stumbled across a shoebox of correspondence from Uncle Eliel. She read from some of them and gave me the first letter Uncle Eliel wrote to her. Mama said I should bring the letter with me to the United States so that I will remember those who are left behind. My letter said . . .

"We are so grateful for your help. We ate meat that day, the first that we have had for over a year. We usually eat only rice and vegetables, sometimes with fruit and, of course, we have our water and salt.

The last time that we ate meat, we found some frogs in the fields. We put on pieces of old clothes—of course, all of our clothes are old, heh-heh—and kerosene in a bottle to make a light. Then we went frog-hunting at night. But, more often than not, we are too tired to hunt at night. When we get back to our barracks, it is late and we are so tired that all we can do is sleep."

My Uncle Eliel's letter mentioned other things but I usually thought about how his family did not have much to eat. Many years later, I conducted some research as an aide to a United States Senator who was being lobbied by Amnesty International regarding certain labor incidents in Negros.

I learned that about 70% of the province's sugar-growing land was located in haciendas, a remnant from Spanish colonial days that has been compared to American's southern plantations before the United States' Civil War. The workers' houses were typically rough-hewn wooden shacks, with no more than twenty-five square yards of floor space. Most families possessed only sparse furnishings such as thin straw sleeping mats and a few utensils. Many haciendas also contained barracks that were partitioned by cardboard walls to house sacadas, seasonal farm workers, from the poor of neighboring provinces. The sacadas were treated the worst among all workers, usually assigned the most menial and harshest jobs such as cutting the cane. I remembered my mother telling me that Uncle Eliel originally moved to Negros as a sacada and never managed to earn sufficient money to leave what he thought would be a one-year posting.

I learned that most hacenderos belonged to a tight-knit political oligarchy. Some were absentee landlords, enjoying the fruits of their wealth in Manila, Hong Kong, London, New York and elsewhere outside of Negros. Some paternalistically defended the hacienda life as the best way of life for the people of Negros who, some hacenderos said, were unable to become self-proficient. At this notion, the representatives from Amnesty International scoffed before adding that, in any event, truly benign dictators would have been less inclined to ignore the widespread hunger and illiteracy surrounding them.

I learned that the landless comprised as much as 98% of Negros' population and that the province's poverty rate exceeded 80%.

I learned that the land reform promised by Corazon Aquino when she overthrew Ferdinand Marcos never materialized and that the landless and impoverished continued to provide fertile ground for labor and political agitation, driven not only by communists but also local priests and nuns responding to the grinding poverty afflicting their flock.

I learned that Negros Occidental was a microcosm of the extreme economic and political inequities that affected the entire Republic of the Philippines. I grew to picture it vividly in my mind as a place where darkly windowed luxury cars drove around malnourished children too hungry and deprived of energy to do anything but mimic puddles on the dirt.

Finally, to finish my research, I tried to live on water and salted rice for as long as I could. I did not last long—a failed experiment that also made me recall the aftermath of the ghost's visit to my home in Baguio City. I remembered once more my consternation over how Uncle Eliel and his family would have hovered on the brink of starvation without my parents' aid. My childhood sense of security had been uninterrupted until my exposure to Uncle Eliel's dilemma as he worked the sugarcane fields of Negros. It was the first time in my life that I felt the ground shake beneath my feet. Uncle Eliel was not a stranger to my family; he *was* family. I never met him but for a long time after the mamau took over Manang Inday's body, I felt Uncle Eliel's presence every time I sat before our dining table.

Ahhhhhh. Delicious, isn't it, my little garbage can, my honey honey bun bun? I would hear his voice behind me as I ate. When I turned around, there would be no one there or only one of the servants looking quizzically at my frightened expression. I came to imagine Uncle Eliel as a diaphanous, floating face with an elongated chin exaggerating the size of his mouth, an open chasm trickling saliva from one corner as he coveted my food. I lost weight that year. It was also the year when, with hunger as my teacher, I first learned how to faint.

Tapey

—after Plato's "The Symposium"

Perhaps Mama should not have become a swindler. But she was bored and tipsy. She also first got involved when she heard the billit, birds, discussing *coitus interruptus.*

"Hah? What are you billit twittering about now?" she yelled from the second-story of my grandmother's house. To avoid my grandmother's disapproval, Mama always drank her tapey, rice wine, on the porch that overlooked my cousin Donna's sari-sari store. The "birds" were the housewives of Santo Tomas who gathered for gossip every evening on the benches in front of Donna's store.

"Non-stop twittering! Just like the billit who eat my star apples off the tree!" my mother disgustedly observed when she first arrived from Los Angeles to begin her summer vacation in the Philippines. She and Papa commenced this annual ritual when my father retired five years ago. But nothing much happens in Santo Tomas, described by Papa as "a town of dust, mosquitoes, tobacco farmers, water buffaloes, and more dust."

Since Papa was born in the nearby town of Galimuyod which competes fiercely with Santo Tomas in regional beauty contests, I knew enough to take his description with a grain of asin, salt. Besides, in response to one of my questions, Mama once described Galimuyod in almost exactly the same terms: "so dusty everyone looks like a bandit with bandanas over their noses, replete with—qué horror!—tobacco farmers spitting on the road, those overworked water buffaloes clogging up the skinny path that passes for Main Street, and—Jesus, Mary, Joseph!—those mosquitoes starving for my American milk-fed veins!"

In any event, Mama often found herself looking for ways to while away these four-month summer pilgrimages. As she frequently punctuated her recounting to me of her brief life as a swindler, "Darling, I'm not a tobacco farmer so I was bored—that's simply how it began! Please believe me, your mother who raised you to be an honest Christian. I did it for the same reason I lapsed into that filthy habit of tippling—Jesus, Mary, Joseph!—Tata Ernie's home-made tapey: I was bored!"

Tata Ernie, my grandmother's next-door neighbor, was infamous for his tapey. He made it according to this recipe which Mama brought with her from her last vacation to Santo Tomas:

> *cook six cups of sweet rice;*
> *layer rice on a flat platter or tray to cool off;*
> *after the rice has cooled, sprinkle with a large fistful of bubod or yeast;*
> *place the mixture in a bowl and cover with banana leaves or foil;*
> *store the bowl in a cool area for about six days to allow the mixture to ferment; and*
> *squeeze the rice through a sieve for its liquid, which is tapey (alternatively, one can forego the sieve since the fermented mixture of rice and alcoholic liquid may be slurped as is from a spoon)*

The key to fine tapey rests in bubod, a mother yeast extracted specifically for making rice wine. Tata Ernie uses bubod from the neighboring town of Suyo, renowned for its sweet variety of tapey. I can attest to the concoction's potency as I allowed myself several glasses to keep Mama company following her first attempt to make it here in Los Angeles where my parents are permanent residents. Mama had successfully smuggled tapey into the United States: it was easy for the custom agent was a Filipino immigrant who happily took two cakes of bubod as a bribe. Actually, Mama offered my glass first to Papa who paled, then replied in a rare display of succinct lucidity, "You're senile if you think I'll drink that!" Then Papa ran away to water the lawn even though the grass was still sodden from a recently-departed storm.

Anyway, as we tested Tata Ernie's recipe my mother said that she was drinking what had become her habitual evening cocktail in Santo Tomas when she heard Innocencia's voice rise out from the babble of gossiping billit in front of Donna's store.

"Jesus, Mary, Joseph! The voice of an angel!" Mama once described Innocencia's dulcet tones. The 21-year-old was newly wed to another cousin, Eddie. Like the spouses of many who gathered at Donna's store every evening, Eddie worked overseas—one of the millions of Filipino contract laborers who labored in Greece, Canada, Hong Kong, Italy, Saudi Arabia, Taiwan and the United States. Their earnings helped buoy up the Philippines' economy which has yet to recover from the plunder caused by Ferdinand Marcos and his cohorts during the Martial Law dictatorship. Nor does the diasporic flow show any signs of easing as the Marcos cronies have returned to positions of power within President Joseph Estrada's administration—returning with the usual disregard for anything beside lining their own pockets despite the continuing poverty of millions.

With the Philippines' inability to fully employ its population and continuing to send hundreds of thousands of Filipinos to other countries, demand boomed for long-distance telephone services. Like Donna, thousands of sari-sari store owners across the countryside installed a phone to accommodate the demand. In Santo Tomas, the spouses and relatives of overseas workers usually gathered between 6 and 10 o'clock every evening to make or receive their calls.

Undoubtedly, Innocencia's angelic voice must have jarred with the phrase "coitus interruptus" so that, for once, Mama paid attention to the tsismis floating up towards where she was enjoying Tata Ernie's tapey.

"Hah? What are you billit twittering about now?"

In response, the birds collapsed into giggles and muffled Ssssshhhhhs. But it was too late. My mother leaned over the narra mahogany railing to peer at the flock whose mirth-ridden faces all looked up at her.

"Oh nothing, Auntie. Nothing . . ." Donna tried to reply but my mother swiftly silenced her.

"I know what I heard! And I know you billit are not conducting Latin lessons down there! What's with this *coitus interruptus*?" Mama thundered.

Before any of the birds could answer, a woman even older than—and hence able to silence—Mama spoke up from the shadows. She limped out onto the light and shook her cane at Mama.

"Betty, where do you think you are? In America? Will you stop yelling *coitus interruptus* to the night air!"

The flock erupted once more into twittering and giggles except for Donna who dashed out from the store scolding the birds.

"Will you all be quiet! Now, here, Nana Doring. Please take my hand and come sit down here where you'll be most comfortable."

At Donna's glare, Innocencia swiftly stood up and offered her spot on the bench to Nana Doring, one of the oldest of the town elders.

"Aaaahhhh. These bones are so tired," Nana Doring sighed as she slowly sat down. Then she looked over the silenced flock surrounding her.

"So. Tell me and Betty over there before she bursts out of either curiosity or tapey: what's all this about *coitus interruptus*?"

As the flock started twittering again, Donna exclaimed in shock, "Nana Doring!"

"What?" the old lady fixed her good eye on my cousin. "I don't know if I should be insulted that you're shocked! Some things, my dear Donna, can never be forgotten!"

This only set off the flock once more on a new round of giggles until Mama yelled again from the balcony, "What about *coitus interruptus*!"

Nana Doring began to raise her cane threateningly towards Mama, but then paused and turned her cane to point it instead at Innocencia.

"So? Answer Betty before she falls and breaks her skinny neck."

"Oh, Ma'am. Oh, Ma'am," Innocencia mustered before her best friend Eva piped up.

"We were just trying to give Miss Newlywed here some advice, Nana Doring. We were suggesting that it's not a proven method for preventing a baby," Eva said.

"Jesus, Mary, Joseph . . ." floated from the balcony but Eva, the least shy of the flock, continued her tale.

"Then Donna said that not only is it not a proven method but it's quite unsatisfactory for the woman."

"Jesus, Mary, Joseph . . .!" this time it was Donna's turn to invoke Catholic royalty.

"So Donna said," Eva insisted on continuing even as Donna began to advance on her.

"Donna said that Innocencia should make sure the man also always fingers *it* so she would not suffer from *coitus interruptus*!"

By the time Eva finished her explanation, Eva was down the road running away from Donna so that, once more, the words floated out onto the night air in Eva's clearly articulated scream towards the laughing flock: "*Coitus interruptus*!"

❧

Thus, did Mama's rapprochement with the birds begin. That evening so amused her that she claimed she lost five pounds laughing with the rest of the billit as they watched Donna chase Eva down the road and then onto the open fields, both women squishing through carabao turds. From thereon, with much whispered warnings to the billit not to tell my grandmother about her evening cocktails, Mama would take Tata Ernie's tapey down to the area in front of Donna's store and join in the gossip.

During one of these evening tsismis sessions, Mama met Innocencia's aunt, Julia. Mama said she never listened to the phone conversations but it was difficult to ignore Julia's turn on the phone that evening. From Julia's side of the phone conversation:

"Now, son. Are you sure it has to be returned?"

Then, "Well, but I don't have it anymore."

Then, "I sold it. What would a humble woman like me do with such a thing?"

Then, after much hemming and hawwing, "50,000 pesos, my son."

Then, several seconds of silence before Julia said, "Fine, call me here tomorrow."

With a deep sigh, Julia gave the phone back to Donna and turned around to Mama's gaze. There is a certain period during all of my mother's interaction with alcohol when the eye she casts on the world is quite unlike her usual nature: during this period, her spirit becomes suffused with generosity so that she becomes concerned that everyone share in the same feeling of well-being she is experiencing. So Mama patted the area next to her and invited, "Come sit by me, Julia. I can see that something is bothering you. Tell me what's wrong."

"Jesus, Mary, Joseph," Julia sighed as she sat down on the bench. "It is so difficult sometimes to be a good parent."

"Jesus, Mary, Joseph—that, it is," Mama agreed sympathetically; then she promptly elicited the tale of Henry, Julia's son who worked as a busboy in the Shangri-La, one of Manila's top hotels. Apparently, about a year ago Henry had found a diamond wedding band and matching earrings in a hotel room. He turned the items over to his manager, a Mr. Carbo, who consigned it to the hotel's Lost and Found. According to the hotel's policies, Lost and Found items not claimed within a year of being reported revert back to the person who found them.

After the year elapsed, Mr. Carbo had called Henry into his office and said, "Congratulations! The item you reported lost a year ago has remained unclaimed. So, as a reward for your honesty, here is the ring which you may now keep."

Henry recalled that he also had reported earrings, but he apparently decided not to challenge Mr. Carbo and merely replied, "Thank you." Subsequently, he gave the ring to his quite gratified mother.

"Oh, my Henry—he is such a loving son!" Julia interrupted her tale and, to Mama's disgust, began to cry. Mama's alcoholically induced beneficence was beginning to wane.

"But Auntie, why are you crying?" several of the billit asked. By then, the whole flock had gathered around to listen to Julia's story.

"Because my boy, being such a loving son, gave me the ring. Jesus, Mary, Joseph—can you imagine? Most would have just sold that thing so he could have money to enjoy Manila which is so expensive! But my Henry is such a good, good boy! He's always thinking of me!"

A chorus of Aaaahhhh's arose. Mama belched, then asked, "So?"

"Well, that was my loving Henry on the phone. He said that the ring's owner has returned after all and wants the ring back, particularly since it is his wife's wedding band."

Once more, a chorus of Aaaahhhh's arose. Once more, Mama belched and asked, "So?"

"But Betty, it's not just a beautiful ring but an expensive one. I can tell. It's real gold because it's stamped 18k in the inside of the band. And there are diamonds all around!"

This time, the flock was silent before Innocencia haltingly offered, "But Auntie Julia, the ring's owner has been found. Surely you must return it?"

"Of course I should return it! But it's not fair that Henry won't get anything for his honesty! Do you know that most people would have just pocketed that ring—just like that Mr. Carbo probably pocketed the matching pair of earrings? Do you know that my son has been engaged to the same long-suffering Lina Asuncia for six years now but that he refuses to marry her until he has saved more money? Do you know how long it will take Henry to save money from that measly paying hotel job? Do you know that we cannot afford to send him overseas to a better-paying job because we can't afford the broker's fees charged by those who would find him such a job?"

Julia paused dramatically, well aware that her audience involved families who had struggled to scrape together such broker's fees.

"So I told Henry that I'd already sold it for 50,000 pesos which I am keeping in a savings account for him," she continued.

"Did you really do that?" Donna asked, undoubtedly voicing the thoughts of the others. There weren't many residents in the region with 50,000 pesos to spend on a ring.

"Of course not! I just made it up on the spot while we were on the phone. I just didn't want to give it back," Julia wailed.

Mama interrupted the ensuing silence with another belch, then asked, "Now what?"

"Well, Henry said he'll talk to his manager Mr. Carbo and call back tomorrow."

The following evening, the flock was larger than usual around Donna's store. Santo Tomas had spent the day discussing nothing but Julia's travails. After all, as Mama often complained, not much else happens in the dusty town.

When it was Julia's turn at the telephone, all the birds stopped twittering.

"Yes, Henry?"

"Yes, Henry?"

"Yes, Henry?"

"Yes, Henry?"

At the fourth "Yes, Henry" Eva groaned but everyone shusshhhed her. Julia continued:

"Yes, Henry?"

"Yes, Henry?"

Julia hung up the phone. She turned around to look at everyone who stared back expectantly. She drew out her silence until Nana Doring raised her cane and threatened, "Jesus, Mary, Joseph! This is not the time to be dramatic! What happened, you silly woman?"

"Mr. Carbo told Henry that the owner is willing to repay 50,000 pesos to my buyer," Julia said hesitantly. "I'm supposed to bring the buyer to the phone tomorrow evening and Henry and Mr. Carbo himself will call again to discuss the matter."

It took the flock nearly five minutes of scrunching their brows to determine what they thought was the significance of this latest development.

Then, almost unanimously, the flock stirred and started clapping their hands in glee.

"But this is great, Auntie Julia!" Eva said. "So you can give back the ring and you and Henry will still have 50,000 pesos! Maybe that will even persuade Henry to stop being so conservative and finally propose to his long-suffering fiancee!"

"You nitwit!" Nana Doring immediately replied. "And who among us would have had 50,000 pesos to buy the ring? Who will play the buyer?"

"That's right!" Julia wailed. "Henry knows none of us can afford to buy the ring. And I don't want my honest son to know I lied, or that I'm trying to swindle anyone out of 50,000 pesos!"

Once more, a chorus of Aaaahhhs rose.

"That's what you get for being such a sly creature." Perhaps my mother only meant to mumble that under her breath but she misjudged and everyone heard her.

Sly Julia looked at Mama. A sly gleam suddenly appeared in her sly eyes.

"But, Betty, you could afford to buy my ring," she said. "You're a balikbayan, a visitor from wealthy America!"

Mama spurted out a mouthful of Tata Ernie's tapey before continuing to splutter, "Hey now, just wait a minute here . . ."

"That's right! That's right! You're the solution to this dilemma," Nana Doring confirmed. "Betty—you shall have to pretend you were the buyer. Henry knows you could easily come up with the money!"

"Wait a minute! Wait a minute here . . ."Mama tried again but Julia interrupted her.

"Of course I should return it!" she repeated. "But it's not fair that Henry won't get anything for his honesty! Do you know that most people would have just pocketed that ring—just like that Mr. Carbo probably pocketed the matching pair of earrings? Do you know that my son has been engaged to the same long-suffering Lina Asuncia for six years now but that he refuses to marry her until he has saved more money? Do you know how long it will take Henry to save money from that measly paying hotel job? Do you know that we cannot afford to send him overseas to a better-paying job because we can't afford the broker's fees charged by those who would find him such a job?"

"Jesus, Mary, Joseph," Mama sighed. She looked around at the billit gazing at her with their pleading faces. She looked at Nana Doring who began to chant, "Betty, I am asking you to do it for me, if not for Julia. Do it for me. Now, who helped to raise you when you were a little girl? Who smashed the head of that snake who nearly bit you when you were a teenager? Who hid you in my house when you snuck out with that loko-loko and your father was angry enough to take off his fat leather belt to give you a lashing?"

"Enough, enough! I'll do it!" Mama cried out.

To cheers, Donna broke out a whole case of Coca-Colas as they toasted Mama's decision to commit a crime. Mama stuck with Tata Ernie's tapey.

❧

In Los Angeles where we sat in Mama's kitchen sharing her first attempt to make tapey from Tata Ernie's recipe, I belched before continuing our tsismis. "Great story, Mama. And the tapey's not bad either!"

"It is a good story, isn't it?" Mama replied smugly, raising her glass to me.

As we clicked our glasses, Mama bragged, "The easiest 60,000 pesos I ever made."

I was about to guzzle down the rest of my second glass (I found tapey addictive) but paused to correct Mama, "Don't you mean 50,000 pesos?"

Mama's eyes twinkled as she downed her glass. I, on the other hand, lowered my glass to the table and repeated, "Don't you mean 50,000 pesos?"

"Jesus, Mary, Joseph. Only 50,000 pesos? Of course I upped the ante to 60,000 pesos."

I stared at Mama as she reached for the pitcher of tapey and poured herself another round.

I managed, "How?"

Mama started to cackle, then took pity on me. She explained:

"The following evening, I got on the phone with Mr. Carbo. I explained that I did buy Julia's ring for 50,000 pesos. I also pointed out that the peso/dollar exchange rate had deteriorated significantly since I made my purchase —another sign of the country's weak economy, you know. So I said I would be happy to re-sell the ring, but at 60,000 pesos so that I didn't suffer any negative currency effect."

After my initial surprise, I began to giggle and choked out, "Ohhhh, Mama! You are cold, cold, cold!"

"Funny—that's what Mr. Carbo said to me," Mama replied. "I don't think I fooled him at all."

"Then I observed to Mr. Carbo: what a shame it would be if the Hotel Shangri-La's reputation suffered from being unable to accommodate this visitor who already had indicated his willingness to compensate me for 50,000 pesos," Mama paused to sip at her tapey. "He spluttered as if I had him physically instead of metaphorically by the balls. But as I expected, after he stopped moaning, he said he would cough up the extra 10,000 pesos."

"But what made you believe he would agree to do that, Mama?"

"Because, darling, I knew he kept the matching pair of earrings that he hadn't returned to Henry who was too intimidated to follow up on it. Believe me, 10,000 pesos is nothing compared to what Mr. Carbo was able to get for those diamond earrings!"

I shook my head and raised my glass to finish the toast.

"To you, Mama," I said and then raised the glass to my lips . . . where it paused before I laid it down again.

"Mama," I said, fixing my eyes onto hers. "I take it that the extra 10,000 pesos was what you got paid for your own complicity in this swindle?"

My mother straightened her spine. She shot me a look from Antarctica.

"What do you think your mother is? Of course I gave the whole 60,000 pesos to Julia and Henry! It's not fair that Henry won't get anything for his honesty! Do you know that most people would have just pocketed that ring— just like that Mr. Carbo probably pocketed the matching pair of earrings? Do you know that Henry has been engaged to the same long-suffering Lina Asuncia for six years now but that he refused to marry her until he had saved more money? Do you know how long it will take Henry to save money from that measly paying hotel job? Do you know that his family cannot afford to send him overseas to a better-paying job because they can't afford the broker's fees charged by those who would find him such a job?"

I still hesitated to complete my toast. After all, I knew my mother well.

"Do you mean you did this out of the goodness of your heart, Mama?"

Mama snorted. "Jesus, Mary, Joseph! How well do you know your own mother? Since when do I do anything out of the goodness of my heart? I did it, darling, because it was something to do and I was just plain bored! Didn't I tell you that there is absolutely nothing to do in Santo Tomas except count the dust motes?"

After a few moments, I sighed and said, "Okay."

Mama looked at me as she took another sip of the tapey.

"Besides, I figured my writer-daughter could use this incident," she said.

"I beg your pardon?"

"I said, I figured you could fictionalize this tale," Mama said, her voice rising in emphasis. Or from tapey. "I thought you could write a short story about this and get it published. Make me proud!"

I was surprised. This was the first time Mama acknowledged my writing efforts without grumbling that writing what she called my "fragile poems and fragile stories" will never pay me even a fifth of what I used to earn as a lawyer for Los Angeles' largest law firm, Carignan, Malbec and Verdot.

"Just be sure, though, to submit your story to places where there are sizeable pockets of Filipino Americans—like California or Hawai'i. None of those fancy-schmancy journals on the East Coast. Submit to publications whose readers can find Filipino grocery stores where they might find the ingredients to make tapey. Oh, yes, of course you must include Tata Ernie's recipe in your story."

My mother belched as I continued to look at her.

I prolonged my stare until she raised her eyebrows and asked, "What? What?"

"Mama. Does this mean you don't mind my leaving law?"

"Don't be silly, darling. Has the tapey gone that swiftly to your head? Of course I mind your leaving a perfectly stable and well-paying profession!"

"Then what…?"

Mama didn't bother to let me finish my question.

"I want you to write this story so that I can bring a copy over to the Philippines. I want to share it with everyone in Santo Tomas."

"Why?"

"Because until your grandmother goes to heaven, darling child, I have to keep returning to that dusty town where absolutely nothing happens! But you can bet that if folks think their interactions with me will get publicized, I might actually start having interesting adventures there! Have you ever tried to count dust motes?"

I looked at Mama. Despite her public crustiness, she really is a good-hearted lady. I know she loves Santo Tomas partly because "nothing happens there"—an attribute she learned to cherish during Marcos' Martial Law reign. She is always bemoaning the plight of the Filipinos who have suffered from crooked or uncaring politicians. She would never admit that she became a "swindler" and refused to accept payment from Julia because she felt sorry for Julia. Julia's family was among the poorest families in Santo Tomas, hence their inability to raise funds for Henry to find work overseas. I also knew that her grumbling about my writing career had more to do with her concerns over my financial security rather than a disrespect for my "fragile poems and fragile short stories."

I raised my glass in a silent toast to Mama before guzzling down its contents. I plopped the glass back down on Mama's kitchen table, belched and announced, "Whatever you want, Mama! Let's hope readers will soon toast us with tapey!"

My City of Baguio

After the century changed its identity, Baguio City are merely two words. Was there ever a house atop a mountain circled by an asphalt ribbon winding its way through happiness? Was there ever a husband, wife, eldest son, middle son, youngest son and middle daughter who was myself as a girl? Was there a housekeeper one pitied for a face so unappetizing she would swallow even an eight-year-old girl's insults? Because ugly women can only return to mirrorless closets and collapse into puddles of cheap polyester. But if the eight-year-old knew that, did childhood really bear no fraying edges? (Was there ever a middle son who died too soon?) Was there really a Baguio City? Ferdinand Marcos: how you confuse me!

·

I believe I once skipped rope in the dining room, though it was forbidden by my parents. But they were looking for gold spilled by the Japanese in their haste to depart when their emperor bowed his head for the first time. And the servants retained vivid memories of aging parents in villages surrounded by dusty fields, empty ponds and mountains blackened by the fires of private armies searching for men who raped their beloveds. So I skipped rope all around our narra dining table until a fly—big and black—bothered me. Inadvertently, I let go of one end of the rope to swat the fly. It betrayed me and became a whip that lifted a vase off the table before smashing it onto the floor newly-burnished with halved coconut husks. And I heard my parents hailing, *Hal-looo,* as they entered through the front door. Maria, the youngest maid, hearing the shattering crystal, had arrived in the dining room mere seconds before my parents. I can still hear the kitchen door squeaking as my mother dragged Maria by her left ear to banish her from the house. It was not the first time Maria took blame for one of my actions; but it was the last time and I remember my eyes were wide but dry as they watched Maria walk out of the door lugging a torn, plastic suitcase.

·

My father has the ugliest feet ever created. I inherited their mere influence and it's enough to make my husband point at my feet and exclaim, *Oh, you're the missing link!* whenever I displease him, say, by chasing yet another white-bearded artist. But I like my father's feet—when bared, they remind me of dead frogs: brown corpses with wrinkled skin and absolutely no hope of moving up the Karmic ladder. What good deed can a frog do except refuse to eat a fly? I like my father's feet because when they move once more I leave the vacuum of pondering the question of frogs and flies. This is why I wish my father would live forever. Because once his feet refuse to move, how would I stop pondering the imponderable: that I, too, am mortal and there are sins for which I inevitably will pay?

❧

Years later, in a country replete with skyscrapers, I will plunge deep into my heart and recall with awe how I never noticed my mother pinching pennies —rather, centavos. Why did I only have one doll? Why was she naked until my mother told one of the servants to sew her a dress from an old t-shirt? *Servants*—is that why I never noticed how often I ate rice with sugar and diluted milk? Because there were always people around sufficiently worse off that I could never do enough to make them stop brushing my hair one hundred times an evening? I felt unaccountable relief at pulling that dress over my doll, smoothing the fabric down past its knees. Why did I never learn to stop asking for more? I did not learn until after my departure that lesser developed countries fertilize strange ironies: when a country is too poor, even the poor have servants and this natural chain can regress forever until one might as well be an amoeba.

❧

My mother frequently took me with her to see movies in downtown Baguio. *Just the girls*, I can hear her say in my memory although I know that, in reality, we were silent as we passed through the door, leaving behind my father equally silent as his dark eyes watched my mother's receding back. In the movie theater, I would watch my mother's legs instead of the torn screen whose stories about blonde characters never folded themselves around my brown heart. I would watch her thighs—how, as she crossed her right leg over her left and, sooner or later, vice versa—her skirt would ride upwards. In the darkened theater, her stockinged thighs would gleam. I would pull her skirt down as much as I could until she pushed away my hands in irritation. Then I would content myself with looking about fiercely at who might dare notice my mother's gleaming thighs. Until my mother pinched me and whispered, *Stop fidgeting*. Then I would settle back into the same rigidity that turned my father back home into a statue. Except for my eyes—like my father's—flickering, watching for what shape the devil next would come in.

❧

The schoolchildren wore uniforms: white blouses and dark blue skirts. Everybody knew to buy skirts with long hems that could be let down as the girls grew taller. No one thought to notice the pale horizontal lines that came to mark the girls' skirts as they moved from one year to another, each parallel line marking a passage from first grade to second grade to third grade and so on. Anna was the tallest child in elementary school by the time she entered the second grade. By the sixth grade, her skirt had a hem the width of her mother's infinitesimal stitches and still the skirt failed to dip much below her panties. But even the black-robed nuns remained silent because Anna had six sisters and their mother was a widow. To this day, I can never wear a mini skirt. Anna's knees were knotted like old wood: rotten to the core like a dictator but quicker to buckle under pressure.

❦

Every week we would be shepherded by nuns into a Catholic Church whose grey spires and cracked stained windows loomed over the plaza of our school. I hope never again to see children's faces as solemn as the sheets encasing my classmates' faces. A reflection does not allow for the honesty of a third-party observation. I believe it impossible not to pose in front of a mirror. I stroked the smooth mahogany of the bench while I waited for the children to flow through the confessional booth. And I would watch them stand in line, their faces battlefields for the attempt to concoct sins they could confess to the waiting priest. To be lacking in something for which the Church could play a role was to be lacking, even though its lack was supposed to be a virtue. Many would look at where I, a non-Catholic, sat, wishing to trade places or at least for an encouraging smile from me. I never met their eyes. I merely traced the smoothened wrinkles of wood and vowed never ever to be so fragile, like the little girls with solemn faces clad in dark blue skirts with undone hems marking their growth. They also wore white blouses, always pristine and usually threadbare.

❦

Whenever we were visited by relatives from the barrio, I always had to share my bedroom. I would wake to old men and women huddled together on thin mats on the floor beside my bed. They were always grateful even when the first cup of coffee was too watery. My parents consistently offered visitors my bed, but no one would displace me—perhaps that's why my parents always offered, even if to my father's brother whom my mother despised. *And where would the angel sleep*, all would brush away my parent's offers. This angel had never known to be uncertain over her parents' offer to sacrifice her bed. How did this come to be—today I happily would give up my bed for the elderly. But the best I still can do about the homeless is pretend to ignore those shoplifting groceries. Where's the consolation? I've seen too many old men and old women sleeping on hard surfaces. How am I ensuring the certainty of never being displaced when what is lost becomes seamless into what is gained?

❦

Black feathers, corn kernels so young their whiteness blinds, an unraveled sleeve, a weeping servant, my father's 30-inch waist, younger brother begging me to decipher a fish head, boiled bone marrows, rhinestones in my mother's eyeglasses, middle brother learning global geography by filling notebooks with foreign stamps, neighbors peeking through the fence, slices of green mango encrusted with salt, oldest brother practicing opera to the household's bated breath. *AND* behind an armchair, I sat silently, a naked doll clutched to my chest, persistently suckling one thumb in my mouth.

❧

Hammer a chasm until it bleeds snow and gravel. Then you'll taste zinfandel by biting your lover's tongue. What does this have to do with me? I am short with flat hair and no flesh on my lips—I am stuck with critical tears. Others have tamed gorillas and hailstorms, rolled bodies safely under waves attempting to topple green-eyed bankers off their surfboards laminated with frozen lightning. Who weeps for discipline when the Midwest lines up to have their teeth blackened by *double entendres*? So hammer that chasm until the head falls off to bounce on a suture and undoubtedly hit me smack between my eyes.

❧

Truly, I was a stupid child. How could I ignore any significance to the placement of my family's house atop a mountain. The views were munificent with magnificence—beyond the living room window one could stare into God's bedroom. Drop a gaze and one could consider the edges of the universe unraveling the suture against a godless black hole. The breathlessness of seeing! Such sheerness! Except for that shock interrupting the path from the bottom of the mountain up to the gates that opened onto my family's front yard replete with bougainvillea bushes. Halfway up and halfway down the mountain, a box leered with peeling paint, broken shutters, a mistress with a voice like fingernails scraping a blackboard and two humongous black dogs with snouts as long as a dictator's lie. I felt such relief at being attacked by those dogs. I had waited so long for the inevitable. But my family never moved from the view into God's bedroom, despite my bandages continuously sprouting red blooms whose petals insisted on widely unfurling. Just when one heard God opening his curtains, a man in Manila mugged the country we shared. Then and only then did we leave that house atop a mountain. Did we overlook so much as we tilted our eyes upward? Like the ants whose nibbles irritated dogs or distracted my family from earthly issues? Like how children define "HOME"?

❧

I never experienced an orgasm in Baguio City. I used to consider this significant until I recalled how I stopped coming when I evolved into a married woman. Is my husband Baguio City? Is that why I married him? No, I married him for his money. But we woke after our wedding night to his question: *I thought you were the rich one.* Then why are we celebrating our tenth wedding anniversary? Because he is Baguio City? Yes, with him, I am a girl again. He may be poor but he is a Jew: he can only take care of me. I followed him to Israel last year and it was no price to pay. If anything, to float on my back in the Dead Sea enhanced my debt to him. Of course, I have debts to Baguio City, too. I would love to repay *those* debts but I can never find my way to return. All those Imelda Boulevards, Imelda Highways, Imelda Avenues, Imelda Streets and they all lead me circling like a vulture over and around the city. But Baguio City, surely, is no stinking piece of dead meat? No matter how much I desire to land, Baguio City is closed to me. And I must simply make do with my Jewish husband whose sole word of Ilocano, Baguio City's language, is "kili-kili." It means, *ARMPIT*.

❧

I grew up in a house enfolded by a balcony to maximize enjoyment of mountainous scenery. The air was as crisp as chicharron, fried pork skin. Below my nose a field of sunflowers sprawled on its knees. I never knew what those golden orbs were begging for. Two decades later, in a garden in Munich, I would be hailed by their cousins and marvel at how much taller sunflowers grow in Germany. Is it that Germanic air that lacks mañana-time? The balcony ended before invading the air over the backyard. In the past I applauded that decision—in the backyard, a faucet monotonously leaked drops of rusting water. Occasionally, the leaks would offer a reprieve to our household, but when the puddles evaporated, their grief would remain through stained cement. Romance never lingered in the backyard, unless you count the feline strays who would pause to lick themselves. But now, I wish the balcony had run its length completely around the house. Then, perhaps, innocence would have remained, unable to unlock its handcuffs.

❧

In Baguio City, I still cared so much. I didn't even balk when Sister Mary Agnes unfurled my clench and laid an empty notebook on my palm. She instructed that I make the pad overflow with descriptions of my daily good deeds. A Good Deed del dia. But why did certain things count and others not? Why did dieting evoke zero applause? Why did my mother wake a poor man around the bend of a path at 2 a.m. (after a party) to offer leftovers? Which act was made in sympathy, surrounded as we were by water buffaloes patiently pulling their masters' carts? Today I have no masters except poetry that turns my heart into a river during a monsoon. Except for those lapses, I don't care much nowadays. Though I regret being accustomed to the dig of my fingernails into the bellies of my palms. When I spill, I notice the stains instead of the diminished source.

❧

I did not know then how cruel mini-skirts can be. Or that words can protrude. It's just as well I left Baguio City before I learned to weep at television commercials; at the same time, I understand why handkerchiefs have become old-fashioned. Sometimes, I console myself by noting my ability to linger on the curve of a woman's blonde breast. That's when my left shoulder laughs at me and replies, *Your heterosexuality is convenient.* Damn convenient.

❧

The house next door has been occupied by a new family. It comes with a spoiled son. He was also the youngest and only male among six siblings. After thirty years of being spoiled he is a circle of a man with a dim and depthless belly. Baboy—that's his nickname from the neighborhood kids. *Baboy.* Pig. All this was of no concern at first; when Baboy arrived I was engrossed in collecting labels off canned goods produced by Marigold Company. For each ten labels, they would donate one centavo to my school. The nuns unleashed their whips. The principal, Sister Gloria Mantulukikulan, hectored us every morning through loudspeakers over the campus plaza where we lined up before filing into class. "Let us help Marigold Company finance new textbooks, children!" Sister Gloria's nose was red with her passion. "Yes, sister!" our voices would float like balloons. My neighbor, *Baboy,* salivated over Linda, a sixteen-year-old maid Mama hired out of charity. *Pssst! Pssst! Baboy* consistently called through the fence when I had to walk by. *Maganda! Who is your pretty sister?* Baboy would query, his snout driving through the chain-link fence as he pushed his chin towards the direction of Linda washing my mother's underwear while enjoying the sun. I dutifully ignored him until he whispered, "I have Marigold labels for you." I introduced them, pinching Linda and ordering her to be polite as she reluctantly accompanied me to the fence. In the immediate aftermath, I used to console myself that at least Linda will never starve. Then things finally died down a bit and people stopped gossiping about how a young girl was compromised enough to marry Baboy. From such small beginnings, much can and did occur. This, after all, is a tale of hunger. There must be a reason why, two years later, Ferdinand Marcos successfully proclaimed Martial Law. And, now, an adult, I can't even comfort myself by the thought of new textbooks for my childhood school—those history books apparently have their facts all wrong.

❧

Twenty-six years later, I am surprised by an old Filipino. He tells me that what I long assumed to be barbaric was actually a sign of sophistication. Nor was it unleashed as a means to extend a finite family budget as the practice actually was expensive. To think I sniffed my nose at it, only once allowing—the portrait of condescension—that its skin, at least, tasted okay after its fur was scraped off and then charred for three hours over a backyard fire. I don't believe ever having tasted its ears, though I imagine the squatters against our backyard fence must have loved it pickled in vinegar and black pepper. It is fortunate that my husband detests cats; I tell him I need one in exchange for a dog he would love to have. Stalemate. I learned to tell the difference between food and a pet. But when I left Baguio to become an American, I left two behind: Brownie and Tigre. I must have known their fate—even though I let the word out in the neighborhood that I would return as a ghost to haunt them if they ate my dogs. What I had not realized was that some might mistake Imelda Marcos as my ghost. So the neighbors ate them anyway, in retaliation for Imelda and her husband tightening the means for an honest livelihood. I never thought Brownie and Tigre would roast over a spit. But, then, I never thought a greedy man would turn my birthland into a classic banana republic because the downtrodden would be unable to afford anger.

❧

I recall the rains. Baguio is pronounced "bag-yo." And the Ilokano word, "agbagyo," means "to storm." I recall walking the streets under an umbrella held over my neat pigtails by one of our maids. I often ducked out to quench a thirst—it was a mystery why my throat was parched by the sight of so much water! —only to be unslaked by those fat drops that loved to evade my opened lips. And I would try to satisfy myself by watching the rain slip-slide down my legs. Afterwards, Baguio City would be green and smell green. And the best part was watching the stall-owners return to Baguio City's open market. They would greet each other as if they hadn't seen each other just an hour or so before. And some would pat me on the head as we waited patiently for them to put their wares back out on display. Others would slip me candy, hushing the maid's faint protests. Soon, my cheeks would bulge like my eyes at the sight of rebirth occuring over and over again. Overhead, the sky would become blue, as it unfailingly did after every storm over Baguio City ended.

Ferdinand Marcos—your red rivers stained more than 7,000 islands. But you couldn't reach the blue blue sky over Baguio City. And now you are dead. In Ilocos Norte, your wife has ordered you chilled in a freezing room. The stupid woman has mistaken you for Lenin. But I know you are underground. And I know it's hot down there. Ferdinand Marcos: I see a blue sky over Baguio City. It could have been the floor of your eternity. Look up now, into my dirty sole childishly stamping on your long nose. And again, know that the sky is blue over Baguio City. The horizon begins with what looks like a cloud, but I know it is the tip of an angel's wing. I hammer you, the chasm behind the suture that is my heart.

The Man In a White Suit

—from "West of Brawley" by Douglas Spangle

"Have you thought of returning?"

I did not need to specify a place when I asked the question of my father. Beyond the window, orange lightning cracked the forehead of the sky stained the color of a squid's blood.

My father turned his face to me and I noticed not for the first time how his hair had whitened. He replied, "Hija, my child, that is a country whose people has done to themselves what once I thought only foreign invaders would do."

I knew then that he would retire from teaching history to continue living in the same city that has been his home for the past 25 years: Stalton, California —the most dangerous city in the United States, according to the latest crime statistics compiled by the FBI, a ranking boosted by the drive-by shootings perpetuated on each other by the city's gang members. In Stalton, the Mayor gnashed his teeth every Monday morning as the weekend's body count arrived on his desk.

But in Stalton, pretty college co-eds were not kidnapped by local policemen or the private armies of rich men, gang-raped and then razor-slashed to ribbons. Nor were half-naked children so bereft of energy from malnourishment that they mimicked puddles on the dirt all day as black limousines drove past them. Nor were men forced to forage in garbage heaps to feed their families. Nor were priests and nuns driven to carry guns like communist rebels.

White suits. My father said he used to wear white, starched suits daily, with a white handkerchief in his breast pocket. He said he also used to carry around a Panama hat with a white band just for show. And the people would exclaim, *Ahhhhh*, and marvel at the dignity of his presence.

Nowadays, most of the men who demanded the respect my father once received do not bother to change before going to dinners or lunches in public places. For the few who did more than wash their hands, white suits were no longer fashionable; dark colors camouflage blood.

But when I would visit Stalton during weekends and sip lemonade while my father tended the rosebushes in his garden and the sound of a car backfiring jumped like a thief over the fence, my father's face would pale into a frozen scream and his hands loosen to let the pruning shears fall. Then I'd stand there with a throat as dry as California's drought-stricken future, watching my father pose like a white marble statue of a naked man.

I would sense through the familiar pangs of hidden tears that my father was hearing the sound of the dictator's minions conducting their latest pillage of that far-away country where mangoes were eaten before they ripened, with much salt and often soaked in vinegar.

"Susmaryosep! Another drive-by," I would hasten to call out, imitating what my mother used to say to comfort him when she was alive.

My father would nod and slowly bend his back to pick up the pruning shears which would just have missed his toes.

"Yes, another drive-by," he would echo and I would sense that he would be comforted from hearing his own confirmation out loud. Then, once more, he would begin to prune his roses, relieved that he was not in a country he did not recognize.

I would sit back down and gulp my lemonade until my tall glass was empty. My hands would shake as they would reach for the nearby pitcher for a refill. I would pretend to wait for the sunset while inwardly battling a hatred for a man I have never met: a dictator on the other side of the world whose cruelty swelled a tidal wave of diaspora that deposited my father into the most dangerous city in the United States—a fate which the man I loved with all my life considered a blessing.

As night would begin to signal its arrival with a crimson radiance staining the horizon, I would watch my father bend his face towards a red rose in full bloom. And as I would think of Rome burning, I would marvel at how the same sun rose and set on all the places where humanity marked their presence in such a variety of ways. And I would consider once more whether man's history blinded the sun, or whether God had known to create it blind at the beginning of time.

Force Majeure

I quickly tired of watching my big toe nudge air. And after finishing my third
bag of fried pork rinds in one sitting while flirting with ancient carabaos
kicking up the dust in front of my grandmother's porch, I decided to concoct
some diversion on my own rather than rely on Mama. She was still engrossed
in deconstructing my grandmother's career as a loan shark.

I was visiting Santo Tomas because Gran was ailing; my mother was
trying to get an advance on her inheritance by determining which villager
owed what. We all expected Gran to greet St. Peter shortly and enter the Big
Post Office in the Sky. Gran had loved to hang out in the post office with a
huge, rattan purse that contained the pesos she would lend at rates
sufficiently usurious to make my otherwise jaded Mama salivate. Since the
northern part of the Philippines had been wracked by hurricanes and
volcanic eruptions over the past five years, Gran had gleaned quite a few
clients from farmers whose crops were decimated by *force majeure*.

But the waiting was tedium. So I told my cousin, Donna, to plan an excursion
to Baguio City. That's how I met Nickie, my husband and with whom I came to
join the illustrious list of Imelda Marcos' afflictions.

Baguio City is the Philippines' "Summer Capital" for its pleasant weather
year-round, even when the rest of the archipelago sweated under a heavy
blanket of heat and humidity. Popular with tourists, it is famous for shops
specializing in wooden souvenirs carved by the artisans of Igorot, Ibaloy,
Bontoc and other tribes living in the mountains surrounding the city. I
thought I might try chasing down a chess set whose carved figures evoked
native tribesmen battling Spanish colonialist invaders. Besides, I needed an
excuse to leave Santo Tomas for a brief period; its sun was turning me as
black as a tobacco farmer.

No, Nickie was not one of Baguio's unemployed actors, bookies or
gamblers who hung about Burnham Park concocting schemes that would
allow them to afford their favorite habit: beer. I first noticed Nickie after one
Romeo Pascual, a bald and rotund lad whose life's ambition was to visit
Graceland, overheard my Americanized English and insisted on making me
the target of fake but immediate adoration. That day, despite the
combination of my overflowing belly and virtually non-existent breasts, I
offered the unique merits of correct citizenship with whom marriage could
provide entry to the land of Elvis Presley's birth.

Nickie came over to the huge acacia tree that shaded the plastic chair
where I sat fondling the chess pieces and nibbling fresh coconut slices as I
concocted for Donna a feminist theory for the Queen's powers versus the
sluggish chess steps of the King. We were also being treated by the
improbably named Romeo to his egregious Elvis imitations. Leave, Nickie
ordered Romeo, otherwise Romeo would find himself doing the jailhouse
rock for harassment, noise pollution and spitting on the ground (the latter
charge being particularly frowned upon by Baguio's earnest cops, according
to a sign by the park's entrance). At least, that's what I assumed Nickie told

Romeo since he spoke in Tagalog, the Philippines' national language that I do not understand, having been born after my parents emigrated from Santo Tomas to San Francisco.

"Thank you, Nicolas," Donna said gratefully. I had been amusing myself by offering smiles and flirtatious glances from beneath my stubby lashes to encourage the lout with the voice of a tuba, or "loko-loko" as Donna muttered under her breath; thus, my cousin was much relieved by Nickie's intervention. Nickie's real name is Nicolas Cosmo Cabiling. I call him Nickie because the diminutive is my way of responding to his irresistible charm.

In any event, as he confronted the loko-loko trying to flirt with my heart and passport, I noticed Nickie for the first time and felt a certain stirring in my loins. I hadn't felt that simmer since five years earlier when I developed a mad crush on Dr. James Pix, my former dentist. Like "Pixie," Nickie had glossy, black hair poorly cut to hang about a narrow, angular face with cheekbones as chiseled and perfectly aligned as those of Ivan Lendl's. Like Pixie (and Ivan Lendl, had he been unable to afford well-groomed hair), Nickie evoked a Russian monk I once saw while playing tourist in St. Petersburg. The Russians were celebrating Easter and I was in church because it was on my tour group's itinerary. Since the monk was both orthodox and behind a cross, I left him alone. Pixie, I didn't leave alone. But after making me suffer through ten dental cleanings in one month, he finally suggested the name of a female dentist who was also covered by Blue Cross; I took Pixie's hint and gave him up. As I watched Nickie increase the intensity of his glare against Elvis Imitator Number 798, I began to shift on my seat from that long-dormant simmer.

"Who is this utterly delectable guy?" I whispered to Donna as Nickie carefully watched my would-be suitor slink away.

Donna looked at me strangely and said, "He's our driver. You sat behind him for six hours from Santo Tomas to Baguio."

Hmmmmm, I thought. He's from Santo Tomas, too. All of a sudden, waiting for Gran to die didn't seem as tedious as before.

❧

The following day, Nickie sat on Gran's dining table decorously sipping the hot chocolate I insisted he try because I proclaimed it was the best Switzerland had to offer. Before leaving San Francisco, I had packed some provisions I didn't expect would be available in Santo Tomas: Mallomars and the Swiss Miss brand of powdered chocolate mix (the latter is actually made in Cleveland but I assumed Nickie would be ignorant of that fact). Nickie was visiting at my request because, ostensibly, I was looking for a driver for another excursion—this time to visit Marcos' embalmed body in one of his childhood homes located three hours away in the town of Laoag.

"It's richer than local brands," Nickie said after a cautious sip at Swiss Miss. Then he smiled briefly at me. In the future, he would admit he didn't care for chocolate but decided it was more prudent to be polite. Nevertheless, he smiled and, though brief, that smile sufficed to make me feel once more that certain stirring in that netherward region of my newly sensitized body.

"So, what do you do when you're not chauffering tourists around?" I asked, crossing my legs and pushing forward a plate of Mallomars. He must have been thoroughly disgusted by the cookies and marshmallowy goo generously encased in thick, dark chocolate.

"I plant vegetables," he said.

Nodding enthusiastically, I brilliantly asked, "What kind?"

"Tomatoes."

"Rea - a - a - ly? How very interesting," I replied and drowned myself in the depthless pools of his brown, brown eyes. His eyes woke me to the wonders of the color brown.

When I surfaced to breathe, Nickie was looking at me as if it was still my turn to speak.

"I beg your pardon?" I breathed, suppressing the urge to fling myself at him and crush my breasts, such as they were, against the muscles evident under his thin, white t-shirt.

"When would you like to visit Ferdinand Marcos," he repeated.

"Tomorrow?" I said, trying to disguise the hope in my voice.

"That's fine," he said, rising from the table. Because he readied to depart, my heart plummeted like an overripe mango from its branch.

I also thought Nickie was an absolutely brilliant conversationalist.

❧

I long suspected Imelda Marcos was off her rocker. Peering at Ferdinand Marcos' body embalmed in wax and lying in a room with a set temperature of 58 degrees, almost half the outside temperature of Laoag that day, I ruminated once more that Imelda should be the one knocking on St. Peter's gate to put the Filipinos out of their misery which, contrary to her frequently touted belief, had never been alleviated by watching her dress up in thousand dollar *terno* gowns and diamond-pelleted rosaries before going disco dancing with George Hamilton.

"Oh my god, oh my god," Donna kept exclaiming as we walked around Ferdinand's body. Imelda must have visited Lenin's Tomb during the years she forced herself into the role of the Philippines' senior diplomat and came to fancy the manner in which the Russians immortalized the guy who unnecessarily killed the Romanovs. I tried to hide my irritation as Donna kept comparing the dead dictator to the most supreme of deities; many residents of the Ilocos region, which included Santo Tomas, still worshipped Marcos who was born and raised in their midst. Totally aggravated, I left the mausoleum to look for Nickie who was waiting with the van outside.

"Bastard," I hissed as I slid into the front seat, still thinking of the man who exemplified Aristotle's claim that absolute power corrupts absolutely.

Seated behind the wheel, Nickie coughed. I looked at him in dismay.

"Sorry. Did I say that out loud? I didn't mean you," I quickly said.

"Did someone offend you?" he asked, staring past me towards Marcos' childhood home. He frowned as if he expected to see the glistening scalp of Elvis Imitator Number 798.

"Oh, no, no. I was actually thinking of the man whose body now lies all decked out in pompous ceremony back there...," I broke off and quickly shook my head, determined not to let thoughts of Marcos ruin a moment with the subject of my dreams. I woke that morning entangled in soaked bedsheets and sucking a raw knuckle.

I looked at Nickie's eyelashes: dark, thick, long—the curl on their tips evoking waves exactly at their peak before breaking to cool a shore of heated sand. Sitting on my palms whose fingers ached to ride those waves, I suggested, "Let's not talk about him. Let's talk about you."

"Why?" he replied, raising an eyebrow (perfectly shaped and as lustrous as a crow's wing, quite unlike the mess of fuzz capping my eyes).

"Oh, I don't know," was the best I could manage. That, and a stupid, silly giggle.

After a brief silence as I nibbled at the manicure that Donna had given me while we passed time on Gran's porch, Nickie said softly as he stared ahead through the windshield, "I didn't care for him either."

Startled, I spit out a Royal Cranberry flake and asked, "Who?"

"Ferdinand Marcos, of course," Nickie said as he looked at me. He smiled and added, "The bastard."

I would insist for years afterwards that it was at this moment that Nickie fell in love with me.

❧

Conveniently, Donna needed to run some errands in downtown Laoag. So we dropped her off as I pretended that I needed to stop by the local airport to check on the schedule of flights to the United States.

"Are you sure you'll be all right?" Donna asked earnestly as I shooed her out of the van.

"I'll be fine," I insisted, waving her off.

"Besides," I added, glancing at the impassive man by my side, "Nickie will take care of me."

After agreeing to meet later at the same spot in three hours, we zoomed away from Donna's sweating face.

It was Nickie's idea to sabotage the electric generator that cooled Marcos' mausoleum.

"Imelda hasn't paid the electricity bill for at least six months. Bastard can fry," he rationalized to my willing ears as we planned our escapade. He pronounced, "bastard," with relish, drawing it out as "baaas - taaard" as if he had never heard of the word before and found its taste irresistible. In response, I opened my lips and found myself short of breath. I still respond the same way today. Sometimes, when he's addressing that certain stirring in my loins and the moon is full beyond our bedroom window, I ask him to say the word: *baaas - taaard*. But I remain too embarrassed to tell him why, no matter how many times he asks me to explain my strange predilection.

I had noticed that the security was quite lax around Marcos' childhood home. Enrico, the guard, was usually asleep—easy enough to determine as his snores were the type to rattle the *capiz* windchimes floating over his station. As for Innocencia, the salesgirl who sat behind a small table peddling old postcards and browning photos of the once-cute-but-now-bloated Ferdinand "Bong Bong" Marcos, Jr., she usually spent the day bowing her head over her crocheting. We tip-toed past the near-sighted Innocencia as shells tinkled to Enrico's vibrations of his soft palate—a symphony that masked any sound from our steps as well as the choked laugh I loosened when Nickie inadvertently kicked a mangy lizard that appeared from nowhere.

The generator was housed in a shack in the backyard. The door wasn't locked and we quickly stepped into the dimness. Nickie confidently opened a box and traced his fingers over the thing-a-majigs that laid there. I knew nothing about electrical circuitries and such but insisted on accompanying Nickie. Though silently bemoaning my eyelashes' deficiency, I couldn't help batting them as I simpered, "Please don't torture me with the suspense of waiting while you endanger your life."

Then I raised a hand (trembling slightly) over my heart as if it was threatening to explode at the thought. Nickie offered a bemused look before quickly looking away. Months later, he revealed that he responded to what I thought was a becoming maidenly fluster by wondering whether the heat or my over-sugared diet had addled me.

After checking a few of the electrical thing-a-majigs, Nickie said softly, "This should be it."

He placed a hand over an orange lever. It was positioned by an "On" sign; pulling it down would position the lever by an "Off" sign.

I placed my hand over Nickie's palm and, with silent apologies to Nike, exhorted in a hoarse whisper, "Just do it."

His hand quivered briefly under mine, surprised by my touch. He looked into my eyes and, this time, I couldn't hide how I felt about him. I've long felt that when we both pulled down the lever, it was the first time we made love.

❧

Much to Imelda's dismay, visitors had long stopped trekking from any of the country's 7,000 islands to genuflect before Ferdinand's waxed body. The man who once claimed it possible for an honest Filipino to earn $10 billion had become merely a tourist attraction in a dusty region with limited competition. The next time Enrico opened the mausoleum, it was five weeks after our visit.

"*Was ist los*, what is wrong?" the German tourists gasped as they entered the room. With its failed air conditioning, the mausoleum's thoroughly sealed walls made the interior hotter than the 110 degrees then boiling Laoag. The mausoleum also offered a stench that a newspaper reporter later likened to "a fruity mix of bananas, coconut oil and star apples underlaid by whiffs of spoiled eggs and rotten frog meat."

"*Qué horror!*" Enrico, who was once gifted Spanish lessons by Imelda, exclaimed and bolted towards the direction of Marcos' body. Clamping their fingers on their noses, the Germans heaved curiously in his wake.

The wax had melted off Marcos' visage, leaving behind a skull with hollowed eyes peering out of the stiff collars of his yellow tunic. Out of each sleeve, the bony fingers looked incongruous against the still puffed out torso. Imelda's cohorts must have stuffed Ferdinand's suit with something more robust than wax to enhance his body's appearance.

After Marcos' stinking—no pun intended—body was discovered, Nickie began stopping by every evening to share that day's coverage by the *Ilocos Bulletin*. I attribute the reduction of my belly to those evenings of prolonged, wheezing laughter as we savored every word of every article. In particular, we scoffed at the photo of Imelda's outraged mien topping an immense bunch of microphones; its caption featured her lashing out, "The Philippines has never known such tragedy!"

"Yeah, right," I pithily mocked her words.

"Baaas — taaard," Nickie agreed, quickening my breath and parting my lips. That's when we shared our first kiss.

❧

I freely confess that I seized on Gran's impending death as the excuse to march Nickie to the altar of Santo Tomas' church a few weeks after our first kiss. For the first time in many months, Gran's eyes sparkled as, seated in a wheelchair bought for the occasion, she watched me walk down the aisle festooned in lace, silk, pearls and pink baby roses. The whole village turned out to cheer one of their sons finding wedded bliss with one who returned to her cultural origins. My bridal gown naturally was dazzling white and, forgetting my difficult romantic past, I was ecstatic I could feel sincere about the color. My happiness was so contagious Mama announced that she was forgiving everyone who still owed money to Gran (I think Mama also finally accepted defeat in deciphering Gran's scribbled records as to which farmer owed what).

Nickie claims no regret over our hasty nuptials, even though Gran has recovered sufficiently to spend her days again wandering the halls of her beloved post office. To Gran's irritation but my amusement, there is limited demand for the contents of her purse. God seems to be in good humor, with nature's moods quite benign of late.

Meanwhile, I have acquired a goat. I tend Bang-Bang while eating raw tomatoes, freshly plucked from the vines climbing our new residence in Santo Tomas. They taste as sweet as Nickie's lips, sweet enough to overcome my dismay at my complexion, newly darkened by the sun that remains consistent in its brightness.

Redeeming Memory

"It takes tenderness to perceive"
—from Poem No. 37 by José Garcia Villa

"Who knows what happens to the prayers we so fervently believed in as children?"
—from "PLANET WAVES" by Eric Gamalinda

"This is the moment in which I am living now: teleology more than denouement, neither exorcisms nor culmination."
—from "IDENTIFICATIONS" by Clinton Palanca

January 1, 1998

Once I thought pity to be the worst emotion one can ever feel: an acidic invasion that easily corrodes the heart. Then I began to doubt myself, wondering whether other emotions bear the weight to scar deeper. To be sure, there's a futility in meandering along the paths of thoughts like these—a survey inconsequential by itself, and as if its conclusion is unchangeable once formed. But I still ponder the role of pity in a ranking of least desired emotions because I am unable to stop doubting whatever conclusions I have ever reached in my life, unable to stop myself from reconsidering once more any thought that I once conceived with the most modicum of certainty. Currently, I believe there is no less unsparing emotion than regret.

I was 21 years old, the ink still wet on my college diploma from Harvard University. I was arrogant with ignorance as well as smug over my recent *Magna Cum Laude*. And I had just begun a job in Washington D.C. as an aide to Senator Robert Fishbone, IV. I shared his other aides' delight in calling him "Fish" behind his back as it encouraged a false sense of intimacy with the Senator whose personality matched an austere face one expects to see stamped on ancient Roman coins. He also chaired the Senate's Foreign Relations Committee and served as the Senate's Minority Party Chairman on behalf of its Republicans. To become his aide, I competed against 4,500 college students across the country scrambling to determine how one makes a living in the world we inherited; to prepare, we had specialized in such disparate disciplines as political science, psychology, history, philosophy, Medieval Studies, physics (both nuclear and quantum) and religion.

"You must be good," Fish's secretary, Evelyn, said, locking her gaze on my startled eyes as she introduced me to the tiny cubicle that I assumed belied the stature of my position. I felt then like I stood on a pedestal and fumbled in my attempt at modesty. It never occurred to me that Evelyn could have been cautioning—not praising—me.

❧

"It's him again," Mary, the secretary I shared with four of Fish's other aides, whispered as she covered the mouthpiece of her phone. It was the third call from Elmo in the past two hours.

I acknowledged defeat and said, "I'd better take it this time. Otherwise, he'll just keep calling."

Mary smiled sympathetically and transferred the call to my line.

"*Magandang umaga*. Good morning," Elmo spouted cheerfully into my ear. I could picture the wide grin that usually scarred his face. I had memorized the gold rim on one of his capped teeth and a blackened tooth just behind it. I met Elmo a month after moving to Washington when I saw him dance in front of the *Washington Post's* building. Naked except for an Igorot g-string and a placard announcing his protest du jour against Martial Law in the Philippines, Elmo cackled as he imitated bad actors summoning rain in a Hollywood B-grade movie. He stomped his feet and ran about in tiny circles in protest against Ferdinand and Imelda Marcos who were being interviewed in the *Post's* offices. He was surrounded by a gawking gaggle of tourists and other passersby as I walked by his performance act. I also remember a cop on the street scratching his nose, but otherwise seemingly inclined to allow Elmo his freedom of expression. That day, I was among the entourage accompanying Fish to publisher Katherine Graham's dining room where we were invited to join the Marcoses and newspaper editors for lunch.

"*Hoy, Pilipina ka ba?* Are you Filipina?" Elmo yelled as soon as he spotted me. I nodded quickly, trying to hide the gesture from my companions.

Fish stopped walking, turned his noble nose towards me and asked, "Do you know that fellow?"

"No, no. Just being polite," I hastened to reassure Fish, Elmo's torso glistening from a hundred feet away. Later, Elmo would explain he had rubbed some sort of jelly over himself to help ward off the winter chill. He also told me he had worn his costume deliberately to embarrass the Marcoses, especially Imelda who then was at the height of pretending their family possessed some type of "blue blood" that might persuade Prince Charles of the British Empire to wed Imee, the Marcoses' eldest daughter.

Fish nodded and continued towards the *Post's* entrance. Fish considered politeness an underrated virtue (he said so during my job interview) and I knew he would appreciate my response. Elmo might look crazed but, in Fish's eyes, he still deserved common courtesy and undoubtedly would have been willing to wait for me to say a few words to an acquaintance. Indeed, *Everyone Deserves Common Courtesy*, proclaimed a cushion in Fish's office cross-stitched by Evelyn; the saying was graffitied by golden thread across a regal red backdrop. I made sure to gesture to Elmo that I had to accompany the others—as if there was nothing I would have preferred most at that moment than to stay and share a long, cozy chat.

I know that even without the false encouragement of that first meeting, Elmo still would have made sure to discover my identity. A powerful politician, Fish was a logical lobbying target by Elmo and other members of the anti-Marcos movement then flourishing in the nation's capital. Since discovering the phone number to Fish's office, Elmo had plagued me with invitations to all sorts of events sponsored by those whose disagreements with Marcos forced their exile.

"Good morning," I replied, ignoring his attempt to speak the Philippines' national language. Since Elmo met me, he always slipped basic Tagalog into our dialogue in order, he said, "to further educate" me. "*Hoy*, a Harvard hotshot but you can't speak Tagalog," he frequently teased while I smiled lamely. Though I was born in the Philippines, I had immigrated as a child. I also was afflicted by a memory whose tendency to lapse has been a consistent source of aggravation.

"I'm sorry I haven't returned your calls. I have to meet a deadline for one of the Senator's projects," I lied.

"S'okay. S'okay. *Pero, darating ka ba mamayang gabi?* Are you coming tonight?"

I muffled a groan. I had forgotten about the joint gathering of anti-Marcos activists and East Timorese rebels protesting against the Indonesian government. Both camps had agreed to meet in a potluck dinner at Elmo's apartment to see if there were ways they could aid each others' causes.

"I'm sorry, but I'll have to work late tonight to meet my deadline," I said, referring to my non-existent project.

"Work on a Friday night?" Elmo's tone conveyed a slight disbelief. "But you have to eat dinner, don't you? Just come over for a break and chicken adobo."

"I'm sorry," I seemed to be making excuses continuously to Elmo. "But, as a matter of fact, I'll probably even work through the weekend."

"Uh, huh," he said after a brief silence. "Well, maybe you can make it to some of our activities next weekend."

"Maybe," I said noncommittally as I began to feel angry at his persistence.

"You know, if I didn't know any better, I'd think you were trying to avoid us," Elmo said with a bark of laughter. "But that would be silly, huh? After all, you're Filipino. Inescapably Filipino, aren't you?"

Subtle, aren't you? I thought.

"And I know, as a Filipino, you must share our concerns about the 'Conjugal Dictatorship' destroying our homeland."

I tuned out as Elmo spouted his familiar lecture about the excesses of the Marcoses. This time, it included tales about Imelda's latest party feting the actor George Hamilton, attended by false European aristocrats who loved to fool Imelda for free caviar and champagne. Soon, Elmo was rushing his words as if he had so much to say and the phone lines were about to die. I dangled the phone from my hand and waited for the receiver to stop emanating sounds.

"You know, Elmo," I said when he paused, "I'm grateful for your invitations, but I'm not sure it's wise for me to attend your meetings when I represent Senator Fishbone."

In truth, Fish wouldn't have cared what I did on my personal time. My duties had no connection to U.S. foreign policy towards the Philippines. When I first met Elmo and his fellow activists, I tried to explain that my domain had more to do with import duties on Chinese-manufactured textiles and the effect of Middle Eastern politics on oil prices—generic American issues that had nothing to do with the Philippines except as Filipino-Americans might like to buy cheap clothes and cheap oil.

"*Ay, hija.* But you've got access," Elmo had spoken on behalf of them all. "You are in a position to do more!"

Patiently, Elmo had courted my loyalties to their cause. But as I begged off once more from another of their meetings, his voice started to crack. For the first time, I could sense the introduction of scorn in his voice. I looked at the phone receiver in surprise, unused to that sentiment coming from him, unused to that sentiment being directed at Harvard-Magna-Cum-Laude-ME.

"Not wise of you to attend? Re-a-ally? You know, this isn't the Philippines under Martial law—it's the U.S. of A. complete with freedom of speech. Shouldn't you be able to exercise your opinions, whether or not they jive with the Senator's? And if he doesn't have any problems with the Marcos dictatorship, what does that have to do with you? You're Filipino!"

"Or maybe," here, Elmo's rising voice threatened to crack, as if the thought was too outrageous to be true, "you don't believe in our cause?"

Elmo probably expected an automatic, "Of course, I do."

Instead, I let the silence drag out before saying softly, distantly, "Thanks for calling, but I have to go."

As I gently laid down the receiver, I wondered whether I managed to extricate myself without being rude. For many years, whenever I recalled that phone call, the matter of courtesy was the only issue I allowed myself to dwell upon.

❧

Perhaps I focused on the matter of courtesy because it was the issue that aborted my position after barely a year in Fish's prestigious office. Once, I explained to an ex-boyfriend that Fish's dissatisfaction with my job performance had something to do with my immersion in textile tariffs and oil prices, activities that did not encourage much human contact. Thus, I was unprepared when I found myself enmeshed in a series of phone calls from one of Fish's constituents. Inexperienced in dealing with the public, in human relationships, I lost control one day.

"Sir, need you be an asshole!?" I queried metaphorically into the phone during what became my last day serving Fish. A second later, I looked up to see Fish standing by my cubicle with a shocked look ruddying his Roman face before it solidified into chiseled granite. On matters of civility, of common courtesy, Fish was implacable. He left me without a word but I wasn't surprised when Evelyn came rushing over with his orders; I already had started to pack my things. Never mind that the target of my query had just finished calling me a "Menopausal Bitch." Never mind that for weeks I had insulated Fish from this same crackpot who thought Fish should submit a bill legalizing marijuana (the merits of this matter not being as relevant as the unfortunate coincidence that Fish's oldest son died of a drug overdose). I didn't bother explaining myself to Senator Robert "Everyone Deserves Common Courtesy" Fishbone, IV. Maybe I really did find the job lacking in soul.

There's only one problem with that theory on soul, or lack thereof. I ended up trading wheat and pork belly futures on Wall Street—hardly an occupation that encouraged spirituality. Fortunately, this period of my life did come with a bit of saving grace: it lasted only five years and I made enough money to retire comfortably for the rest of my life. My innate predilection for mouthing off flowered because it was a major asset in the trading pits, along with a gusto for flinging out elbows amidst the pack of jackals called commodity traders.

Thus, I was retired by the time I picked up *The New York Times* in February 1986 to discover that Filipinos were using their bodies to stop tanks in Manila. Desperate to retain power, Ferdinand Marcos had won the recent presidential election through ballot-rigging and his goons' murderous intimidation of election overseers. But his Defense Minister and reform-minded leaders of his military banded together to end his reign. In response, Marcos ordered his military to the dissidents' headquarters to squash the rebellion. When word of Marcos' orders spread as quickly as malicious gossip, people streamed out of their homes to form a barricade of flesh, flowers and tears to protect the rebels who had come to speak for the long-silenced majority of the country's population. I would have bet my fortune that would never happen. I would have bet anything that Filipinos would have rolled over and played as dead as my homesickness then for my birthland.

But first, an equally momentous event occurred before Manila grabbed universal attention with its "People's Revolution" that later inspired burgeoning democratic movements in other parts of the world. A man declared, "The Filipino is worth dying for," then proceeded with grace and courage to his death. On August 21, 1983, Benigno Aquino returned to the Philippines from exile in the United States. His first move upon setting foot on Filipino soil was to bleed as a gunman shot him on the tarmac of Manila's airport. To this day, no sane Filipino believes the gunman was not hired by Marcos or one of his minions.

When I heard of Aquino's death, I was saddened but didn't grieve much. I didn't know the man. And what impression I had of him was that he was part of the status quo that gave rise to Marcos. There was a saying bandied about by many Filipinos for years after Martial Law was declared on September 22, 1972: "If not Marcos, someone else would have done it." Such was the nature of Filipino politics, as I understood it. Such is the nature of greed, as I believe it possible.

But my cynicism fell flat in the face of the February 1986 People's Revolution. Under the spotlight of a hot sun, Filipinos walked to Epifanio de los Santos Boulevard and laid themselves across the paths that the military tanks were directed to cross. The Epiphany of Saints! Bankers, students, farmers, nuns and priests, fashion designers, politicians (including former Marcos supporters), slum dwellers, even socialites (in full make-up, of course) all gathered together to spurn Marcos. Faced with their courage, some of Marcos' soldiers began defecting; but even those who remained loyal were reluctant to shoot. I recall a particular photo from the coverage of those days in Manila: a girl in a white dress offering a flower with bruised petals to a soldier grimly staring over her head, his hands clenched around the butt of his rifle, his head capped by a camouflage helmet. The soldier avoided the girl's eyes. Though the photo captured a moment in time, I could swear I detected a trembling, an uncontrolled quiver, about the soldier's seemingly rigid jaw.

Consequently, I became like any radicalized convert to a cause, to an ideal. Since February 1986, I have volunteered my time and income to all sorts of causes that would improve the standing of Filipinos worldwide. Primarily, I am interested in those forced to leave the Philippines in order to earn a decent livelihood. During the 1960s when I was a child in the Philippines, the country's population was just over half the current number of about 70 million people. It is no wonder that people are compelled to leave the shores of their archipelago for the most menial work that could exist in London, New York, Hawai'i, Madrid, Bahrain, Munich, Los Angeles, Melbourne, Chicago and so on. For many, such migration was the only way to ease the burden caused primarily by Martial Law's mugging of nearly two decades of economic progress.

I took my cue from Wall Street legend George Soros whose trading acumen in the world's currency and other financial markets created a personal fortune of $2 billion. George used his money to create the Soros Foundation, a trust through which he funnels grants and loans to aid the economic development of Third World countries. I didn't make anything near a billion dollars but it was enough for me to create the Silang Trust. I named the Trust after Maria Josefa Gabriela Cariño Silang, a Filipina general who led other revolutionaries battling Spanish colonial rule in the Philippines; romantically, I thought to continue her work to improve the lot of Filipino people through the Trust. The Trust's activities have ranged from paying medical bills for workers without health insurance to successfully lobbying the government of Bahrain to forego a death sentence that was imposed on a sixteen-year-old Filipina maid who inadvertently killed her employer while fending off an attempted rape.

Since February 1986, I and the Trust's sole employee, Lisa Soriano, a third-generation Filipina-American and lawyer, have monitored abuses of Filipino migrant workers and intervened where we could. Two years ago, the Trust started receiving awards every few months from human rights organizations, political societies and Filipino community organizations around the world, including a citation for humanism from Amnesty International. Inevitably, I must have developed some complacency over the virtues of my work that encouraged me to feel some measure of relief from having rebuffed Elmo and others then working against Ferdinand Marcos' regime during the early 1980s. At the peak of my psychological security—of patting myself on the back for my wonderful behavior as a philanthropist and human rights activist—1995 arrived and brought with it the case of Flor Contemplacion.

An expatriate domestic helper stationed in Singapore, Flor was charged by the Singaporean authorities for allegedly killing Delia Maga, another Filipino maid, and Delia's ward, a four-year-old Singaporean child. Her death sentence rallied Filipinos around the world in common protest; from Manila, the Philippine government also objected as they tried to introduce evidence discovered after her trial that purported to show her innocence. In Flor's hometown, their words replicated in newspaper accounts worldwide, Flor's children insisted their mother (who barely topped 100 pounds) would not know how to feel sufficient hatred to choke another person to death.

Flor's children added for emphasis, "*Hindi magbubuhat ng kamay sa bata ang Inay!* Mama never would harm a child!"

As soon as we heard of Flor's plight, Lisa and I called everyone we knew at Congress and the State Department. I even called Fish who was sufficiently civilized, notwithstanding our last encounter, to assign a senior aide to try to persuade the Singaporean government to reopen Flor's trial. I don't know whether Flor was guilty of the crimes she was accused of. But she became bigger than her own life. To many Filipinos, Flor exemplified the dangers faced by migrant workers—a major concern as the workers' repatriated earnings created more income than any domestic industry in the Philippines. That was good enough for many Filipinos—and me—to leap to Flor's aid.

We failed. In March 1995, Flor was hanged. I still mourn. Sometimes, the most unexpected pieces of my environment remind me of Flor: a dishrag, because Flor once must have wielded one; a floating cloud, because once, one, too, must have passed over her; a chocolate bar and a bowl of ice cream, because I hope that Flor once must have tasted of their pleasures; and even a mere bar of soap because Flor, too, must have cleansed her body as I do. And I hope that there have been other sources of gentleness for Flor besides her own hands palming her own flesh.

If my involvement in Flor's life and death had any consolation, it was that her death reintroduced me to Elmo, then known more prominently as Eluard Movera, the Philippines' Minister of Foreign Affairs. As I lobbied to overturn Flor's death sentence, Elmo investigated the actions of the Philippine Embassy in Singapore. Apparently, its officials had been too busy planning the embassy's next cocktail party to listen to Flor's pleas from Changi prison, resulting in the failure to introduce evidence during her trial that might have exonerated her. Elmo later fired the Ambassador on duty and replaced virtually all of the staff.

In any event, the Singaporean government held to their original court ruling. Shortly after Flor's death, Elmo sent me a letter on official stationery from Malacanang Palace where the heads of government maintain their offices. I share two sentences:

"Hija, at least you tried to use your Harvard training for something worthwhile. Now, how is your Tagalog?"

Actually, the three-page letter was written totally in Tagalog which I know Elmo designed on purpose. I didn't begrudge his transparent lecture on learning and practicing Tagalog. Instead, I expanded my library with the latest edition of *Tagalog For Peace Corps Volunteers*. If Peace Corps volunteers can do it, so can I, I insisted to myself. To this day, I still try to transcend a weak memory that makes it difficult to learn new languages.

❧

As much satisfaction as I gained from Elmo's letter—symbolizing, I believed, that he forgave my youthful indifference during our days together in

Washington D.C.—I felt more pain from the news that confronted me a year after Flor's death. According to the media, Elmo had absconded with about twenty million pesos, the equivalent of nearly USD500,000 raised by concerned Filipinos around the world for Flor's cause.

I couldn't believe it, and yet Elmo had disappeared from the Philippines. Rumors of his sighting began popping up like weeds through sidewalk cracks, often depicting him escorting tall, thin women in the nightclubs of Argentina, Dubai, Monaco and other countries with whom the Philippines shared no reciprocity laws that would have encouraged their governments to return Elmo back to a ready lynch mob in Manila. In the beginning, I doubted the veracity of the charges against Elmo because I could not forget the passion of his protests against the corruption of the Marcos regime. Also, half a million dollars, though a decent sum of money, can hardly finance a civilized lifestyle on the run almost anywhere in the world.

But then other discoveries were made about the "irregularities" of the Ministry of Foreign Affairs while headed by the man who long had bemoaned my inability to speak Tagalog. There was the alleged bribe by the American engineering firm, General Engines, for receiving permits to build a power plant in Zamboanga. Then there was Virgin Paradise, a resort built out of the former American military base in Angeles City; Virgin Paradise was supposed to be developed by the low bidder in a competitive bidding process but government investigators discovered that the winning consortium was awarded the job because its second-highest price (among ten bidders) included a kickback to Elmo. Other instances of fraud were discovered. Suffice it to say that Elmo, after all, did abscond with enough funds to support a luxurious life on the lam.

When news of Elmo's hidden life first hit the headlines, nearly everyone I knew was aware of our past relationship; in the previous months, I often had ruminated loudly and verbosely—indeed, pretentiously—on the nature of redemption, dredging up my history with Elmo as some sort of example to various points I would make, ranging from "it's a small world" to the unpredictability of fate. As Elmo, my publicly touted proof of uncompromised idealism, became revealed as no better than a common thief, I began to look like a deluded fool. First, there was my quick leap to his defense, then my agitated insistence on his innocence even as his flaws began to be publicized and finally my emphatic notion that Elmo's downfall is ultimately without insight as regards the overall Filipino character. Yes, *Filipino character*: this, too, is as much the cause of my ruminations today—a new day of a new year—as the difference between pity and regret.

Lisa once asked, "How does it feel to have one's god show off clay feet?"

And this tale, too, is my attempt to answer Lisa whom I answered the first time with mere silence.

❧

I began life in the Philippines, living there for years before Ferdinand Marcos declared Martial Law. Until my family immigrated to the United States, we lived among the hills and mountains of Baguio City, a popular vacation spot for its pleasant year-round weather. Atop one mountain, my father built a house encircled by balconies whose views of dawns, sunsets and neighboring expanses were enough to make a child believe the peak of the universe was where the child chose to stand.

My father also built a road from the bottom of the mountain to the front yard of our house. The cement road was a bright symbol of modernization, a first in our neighborhood then entwined in dirt paths. There is a jewel of certainty within my childhood memories: when I left the Philippines, the country was on the brink of immense progress with a wondrous future awaiting its people who had survived many wars and enemies who had invaded its shores.

The Republic of the Philippines. The first modern Asian nation to stage a national uprising for independence when it revolted against Spain in the nineteenth century. A nation where Lapu-Lapu is a household name for having hacked off the head of that Portuguese colonizer bearing a Spanish flag, Ferdinand Magellan. A nation where Filipinos fought in what historians have called "America's First Vietnam" at the turn of the century, battling better-trained men who called them "niggers" as their politicians refused to recognize the independence that they won in a genuine military victory over Spain. A nation where guerillas from the mainstream population consistently fought the Japanese during the World War II occupation. A nation with a history of dying for ideals, for respect, for honor. This was the country of my birth.

How could I reconcile what I remembered as my birthland with the enemy that came from within and the country that was raped and pillaged by a home-grown dictator and his court? I only could lay the blame for what decimated my childhood land to the people who lived there—how could they allow the Marcoses their cruel frolic! I didn't care if I was blaming the victim: how could the contemporary Filipino be so weak? It could only be explained, I felt, by national cynicism: *if not Marcos, someone else would have done it*. If the Filipinos were too cynical, too weak, to overthrow Marcos, why would I bother to enslave my heart to this goal? Didn't I work hard for my escape route from turning that ultimately useless question into my life? I, whose Magna Cum Laude from Harvard University allowed me to compete in a more mainstream part of America than that which concerned the small minority struggling to halt the pillage by that "Conjugal Dictatorship" composed of Ferdinand and Imelda Marcos? For, despite witnessing the efforts of Elmo and his fellow activists, I considered their number inexcusably tiny—not representative of the Philippines' booming populace.

When I met Elmo in 1980, I had not been in the Philippines for nearly two decades. An ocean away, I observed the glory days of the Marcos regime and wondered at the extent of suffering the Filipinos could bear. I was utterly surprised by the February 1986 uprising since I had seen no clues foretelling the courage that manifested itself into scenes of boys baring their chests in front of army tanks and girls draping Sampaguita blossoms over the muzzles of raised rifles—with no one knowing who was more scared at either end of these confrontations.

"This is just a phase—god is merely tired or bored enough to stir things up a bit, to play a joke," I answered Lisa's question the day after it was asked, after a night spent trading baleful glances with the moon which had insisted on being inappropriately bright beyond my window.

Then my good friend, George Soros, called. George and I had become friends after I requested his help in locating contacts who might help Flor Contemplacion.

"I know where the idiot is: Ulan Ude," George announced. I nearly dropped the phone.

"U-where?"

"Ulan Ude. The Buddhist capital of the Soviet Union. Somewhere in Siberia," he replied impatiently. The Soros Foundation had a strong presence in Eastern Europe where Hungarian-born George had spent over a billion dollars since 1989 trying to transform the former Soviet block into thriving democracies. Consequently, George knew anything worth knowing in that part of the world.

"What the devil . . ."

". . . is Movera doing there? I know, I know," George interrupted. A busy man, George rarely has time for others to finish their sentences. "It's convoluted. But he got hooked up with Paolo Denisovitch in some foolish countertrade deal. Something to do with exchanging Filipino tobacco for salmon."

I was stunned. Even I had heard of Paolo Denisovitch, a Russian Mafioso leader enamored with Italy, hence his adopted first name. The guy was infamous for his random acts of cruelty and violence: your best friend one day, then the next day perhaps the guy who'd shoot you for wearing a shirt that offended his sense of fashion design.

"I know, I know," George continued as if I'd spoken. "But Movera apparently got bored sitting on his ass wherever he was holed up in Poland, according to one of my contacts. That, or does he have a passion for salmon?"

The tale was getting more surreal. But that's how I found myself staring at a monk on the Siberian steppes while the wind blew furiously around us. I raised a hand to shield my eyes against the dust while his red robe fluttered about us like a long flag. Around us, the horizon disappeared into a brown shimmer of air that seemed distant one moment, then a few feet away, then distant once more.

"We do not know this person," the monk gently shared through an opening in the ornately carved wooden gate that separated us. Behind him, shacks painted in turquoise, orange and yellow dotted a compound that comprised the monastery. In the distance, Buddha sat on the dirt, surrounded by frozen white tigers rearing towards the white-grey sky. A goat picked its way through the statues.

Can we ever really know someone else? I thought before shaking my head to erase the question's distraction.

"Please. If Elmo, Eluard Movera, is around, just give him this note," I insisted, shoving through the gate an envelope with a note requesting a meeting at my hotel.

"We do not know this person," the monk repeated, but took the envelope. I smiled as ingratiatingly as I could muster as I backed away, back into the hired car that returned me to my ugly, old hotel surrounded by equally ugly buildings of cracked concrete interrupting the vast expanse of the tundra.

❧

The hotel served egregious vodka, but at least it wasn't diluted. I was halfway through the unlabeled bottle when Elmo sat on the stool beside me.

"The monk said they didn't know you," I said in greeting as I looked him over and pretended I hadn't been searching for him for months. He had lost all of his hair, but his wide grin remained. I noticed several gold-capped teeth that were new to me. I also noticed that the mirth on his stretched lips did not, unlike years ago, extend to his eyes. His eyes were dark and black, like silenced mirrors.

"The monk told the truth. And you've gained weight," Elmo replied, faking insouciance as he beckoned to the bartender.

"I'll take a glass so I can save the lady from further polluting herself," he ordered before looking back into my avid eyes.

As I watched him help himself to my vodka, I raised my glass and asked across its rim, "What are we doing in this crummy bar, Elmo? What are you doing here? Poland, then Siberia?"

"Poland. Siberia. Manila. What's the difference, *hija*? With your Harvard training, haven't you learned that we now live in a global village?"

I didn't feel like sparring so I went straight to the point, for the jugular: "Why?"

"*Ay, hija*," Elmo sighed, then drained his glass. I noticed he didn't even wince from the taste that combined grass and petrol.

He refilled his glass before continuing, "Do you remember February 1986?"

"The People's Revolution? The yellow that covered Manila's streets as the people wore Corazon's favorite color? Corazon Aquino leading the crowds in prayer? The girls offering flowers to soldiers? The nuns pleading with soldiers? The soldiers refusing to shoot?"

"Okay, okay. You remember," Elmo interrupted before my voice threatened to rise further. Already, the bartender had tossed us a certain look.

"But do you, Elmo, remember?" I said, softening my tone.

"I remember more than that. Goddammit, I do remember more than that!" Inexplicably, Elmo turned a look of fury at me. "I remember much more than you'll ever know, Ms. Armchair Participant!"

Armchair Participant.

"Ms. Monday Morning Quarterback!" Elmo hissed, before gulping another mouthful of vodka.

Monday Morning Quarterback.

Staring into his glass, Elmo continued in a tone losing its anger to despair.

"I remember—I know!—much more than you'll ever realize from the comforts of your renowned Silang Trust office on Fifth Avenue. I was there, remember? I spread my coat on the ground for Corazon Aquino to walk on as she entered Malacanang Palace. I was there! On behalf of those who didn't live to see February 1986, I held open Malacanang's doors for her!"

I could feel the vodka narrow my vision and turned the beam of my eyes onto Elmo's profile. A lone tear was coursing its way silently down his cheek but he seemed oblivious to its flow.

"Why?" I repeated, not bothering to correct his misconception about the location of the Trust's offices.

"*Ay, hija.* Who knows? Why not?" Elmo began to fumble through his words. "You spend your life fighting for something and watching your closest friends, what became your only family, die for this same goal. Then the revolution succeeds and all of a sudden, you're the one holding court, the one in control of an army, even the one determining fucking taxation policies, for shit's sake!"

Obscenity was unlike Elmo, at least the Elmo I once knew, and I allowed him the respite of another gulp. Then I repeated once more, "Why?"

"Why? Why? Is that the extent of your Harvard vocabulary?" Elmo flared again and looked at me. But, just as quickly, he turned away from the search in my eyes. He continued half-heartedly, :The least you can do is say the word, *bakit. Bakit.* That's Tagalog for 'why,' *hija.*"

"Okay," I said. "*Bakit,* Elmo? *Bakit?*"

He responded by refilling his glass and staring into its depths. Unexpectedly, I sighed and the sound of my breath exhaling loudly jolted us both.

"*Bakit?*" he repeated, then continued haltingly. "*Hija,* we tried to oust Marcos' collaborators—those who participated with his looting of the country. But who replaced them? People of the same character. Or the same people after a while. Do you know that land reform has failed? Now, the yuppies have taken over but we still can't feed our own. We still have to export our college graduates to clean the bathrooms of the universe."

I still didn't have the answer to my question, so I asked once more, doggedly, "But why did you . . ."

I stopped. Unexpectedly, I felt a strange reluctance to state his crimes out loud. I felt it would have been like allowing a foul stench into the room. So I compromised by repeating yet again, "Why? *Bakit?*"

He turned to look at me. This time, he held onto my gaze. His voice was calm as he replied, "Why? Well, *hija,* it can be as simple as the difference between rebelling and governing. To be a revolutionary, one can afford—one must have—the full passion of idealism. I suppose I didn't expect that to govern means being able to compromise—or compromise so much."

Elmo paused, searching me for a sign of understanding. But I kept my face impassive. I couldn't feel anything, found myself untouched by his words. Inexplicably, I was feeling an immense sense of *deja vu.*

He sighed and returned his gaze to his glass. For a moment, he gestured as if to smooth back his hair, only to remember he had lost them all. He continued in a resigned tone, "I only tried to be the best among the rowdy pack of politicos jostling for the most benefits, the highest leverage, in the new government after we kicked Marcos' ass. The slope of compromise, the slippery slope . . ."

Abruptly, Elmo slammed his hand hard on the bar, waking the bartender and the other lone customer at the end of the bar. He held up his glass to me in a mock toast.

"But why am I telling you this, Ms. Armchair Participant? Why do I need to answer any of your questions?"

Then he swallowed his drink in one unflinching gulp, sneered at me once more, tossed a mess of rubles on the counter, stood up, turned on his heel and left.

I forgave him because, for a moment, the black mirrors of his eyes cracked and I thought I saw a flash of raw pain, a jagged lightning bolt—all fury but with the inevitable whimper of mere disappearance against a depthless, dark sky.

❧

The difference between pity and regret is simple. Pity is pity, as untranslatable as poetry; it also can arise inexplicably, be birthed by the most random of circumstances as diverse as pitying someone for being an accountant to pitying a species facing extinction to pitying a shoreline disappearing under the inexorable approach of a sea. Regret, however, is a proactive reaction: a response caused first by an act made or undone by the person feeling the emotion.

I should recount some of the other things Elmo shared about the Marcos dictatorship besides the relatively trivial incidents about Imelda courting Prince Charles for her daughter's hand or the parties for George Hamilton attended by fake royalties who took advantage of the social-climbing Imelda. For instance, how Marcos and his friends and relatives monopolized entire agricultural industries that forced numerous small farmers out of business. This development also boosted the slum population of Manila. Families migrated from the countryside only to forage for food in the city's mountainous trash heaps.

Individual companies, too, were stolen, their assets becoming private checking accounts for those who enjoyed Marcos' favor or for Imelda's legendary shopping sprees throughout the world's most expensive bazaars as well as for buying up prime real estate properties in Manhattan.

There was also Imelda's predilection for creating rosaries from double-carat diamond stones which were often purchased from the proceeds of the latest loan from the International Monetary Fund or donations from the Red Cross for the victims of typhoons, volcanic eruptions, hurricanes and other natural disasters. Thousands have died unnecessarily for Imelda to afford this hobby.

Then there was the island of Calauit in the Palawan region of the Philippines that was turned into a private Disneyland by Ferdinand Marcos, Jr. Since returning from a safari in Africa, the dictator's son had been bored. After a nationwide survey by his equally bored companions, they found an island that was perfect for turning into a hunting ground where the men could wear tailored fatigues and the winners of beauty contests lounge about in tightly cut leopard skins. Unfortunately, creating this playground required displacing the island's residents for the imported giraffes, elk and other animals at which Marcos, Jr. could point his guns. Many of the displaced islanders ended up dying of starvation, unable to find livelihood elsewhere.

The country's youth became dispensable in a land where laws were defined by one's relationship, or lack thereof, with Marcos or his cronies. I recall a pair of college sweethearts, Maria Chavez and Tony Besa. She was pretty and charming and he adored her. She also attracted the attention of a local politician, Assemblyman Edgar Fuentes, who earned his position by once having served as one of Marcos' bodyguards. Assemblyman Fuentes lured Maria to his office by dangling the offer of a rare job. Hours later, when Tony visited the Assemblyman's offices looking for the woman he intended to marry, he walked into a gangbang in progress. The Assemblyman was enjoying his beer and cigarettes, having long finished with Maria Chavez and the last of his six hangers-on was just beginning his turn. The next time the grieving parents of Maria and Tony saw their children, it was after shovels dug through unmarked graves to reveal bodies whose decompositions failed to mask the previously perpetrated trauma. As one of Marcos' favorites, Assemblyman Fuentes was immune from justice; indeed, he perpetrated similar crimes on other, equally young women and those who went to their defense.

The list of crimes perpetrated by the Marcos dictatorship has not yet been completed, an end that may be as impossible to grasp as the ever-shifting horizon ringing the Siberian steppes.

In other words, my rationalizations about cynicism were just so much palaver, much like a famous football player who beat his dead wife out of self-defense. *If you are not part of the solution, you are part of the problem*, Elmo and other members of the anti-Marcos movement used to tell me during our days together in Washington. To understand their words only after nearly two decades is to feel the pulsating scar on my heart, ever raw, never healing, ever raw. Whenever I find myself monitoring its throbbing, I also inevitably recall one of my childhood memories. The first time I remembered this particular memory was in response to the news of Benigno Aquino's death. However, I didn't feel its full measure until that moment in time when Filipinos exposed their hearts to the M-16s and Browning Automatic Rifles being wielded by Marcos' soldiers in February 1986.

This memory is from when I was six, perhaps seven, years of age. I was visiting my grandmother. After a day of frolic with my brothers and cousins, we all gathered together for the evening on the wide floor of our grandmother's living room. My grandmother guided us to a sleep bereft of nightmares as she recounted tales of funny and friendly ghosts: skinny ghosts who love to tickle mischievous children, winged ghosts who look for children who stray from their parents and plump ghosts whose restless fingers loved to pinch the cheeks of children who eat too much. Then there was her last benediction for the evening which often had nothing to do with the benign warning of the tales just ended. *Individual sticks are easily broken*, my grandmother would counsel. *But when bundled together, a different matter.*

For a few weeks after visiting my grandmother's house, I would remember her in the nightly prayers my parents tried to instill in us as a habit. I would pray, my parents watching as I kneeled before my bed, *Please Lord, allow me to be part of your blessed bundle. Don't let me—* and here I would recite a litany of my brothers' and cousins' names—*be individual sticks, easily broken.* I recited words like these until something else came up to inspire and amend my childish nightly prayers.

❦

Armchair Participant. Monday Morning Quarterback. That's me. I once read somewhere that only in our childhood do we create our gods. By simply dozing on the sidelines, failing to file a single protest against Ferdinand Marcos as his regime decimated the landscape of my birthland, I failed to protect my childhood gods. Nothing I do now can make up for that loss of commitment.

I can only search for redemption through my work with the Silang Trust. My grandmother never addressed the possibility of some sticks falling out of the bundle and whether the remaining ones would be strong enough to survive. What I do know and honor is that Benigno Aquino gave up his life for the Philippines in 1983, and that Filipinos united in 1986 to overthrow Ferdinand Marcos. Though Elmo broke, I need not. There are still plenty who can benefit from my efforts. For example, there is a group of Filipino seamen in Mexico who were dumped there by a shipping company that reneged on its agreement to pay them and return them to Manila. Lisa just informed me that, with the help of Senator Robert "Everyone Deserves Common Courtesy" Fishbone, IV, the Mexican government has freed the seamen from the prison they found themselves cast in as illegal aliens.

Finally, to maintain my fortitude in exercising my love for my people who find themselves cast about in all sorts of strange and sometimes unwelcoming corners of the global village, I have renewed an old habit: before each night begins, I pray.

Pork

Camille, Camille…how my husband loved you! You are forever a part of him…

❧

The sight of a man of my husband's age strolling through Santo Tomas with the adolescent Camille could have been misconstrued as a matter of economics—how else to explain an otherwise illogical December-May affair with the added colonial insult of the parties being an American man and a Filipino woman? But for my husband, Tom, the issue truly was one of spiritual engagement. Indeed, he loved Camille with such a purity of affection that, even at my most exasperated moments of their affair, I found it difficult to begrudge their relationship.

Once, strolling through the open-air market of the nearby town of Candon, Tom paused by an array of ribbons laid out like fragments from a rainbow on one of Nana Deling's old bedsheets.

"I think Camille would enjoy the pink one; she is quite girlish after all," Tom noted to the old lady squatting among her wares.

Nana Deling lifted her good eye at Camille who was rooting among the ribbons, spat a wad of tobacco at the ground, but otherwise said nothing before concluding the sale. Everyone in the area had heard of my visit with the *'kano* husband. Perhaps due to the local esteem given to my grandmother, the locals were reluctant to criticize Tom and remained silent on what Tata Bino called his "idiot-syncracies."

No one in the area commented as Tom lovingly tied the ribbon around Camille's thick neck. I concentrated on avoiding other people's eyes—I cringed at how I imagined them pitying me for suffering through my husband's infatuation with a younger Filipina.

Tom and I lived in New York. A few years ago, my parents started returning annually to the Philippines. I usually accompanied my parents on my own given Tom's heavy workload as a Wall Street lawyer. We often stayed with my grandmother in Santo Tomas where I was born 40 years ago. For this visit, however, Tom tagged along to see the land of "luscious Filipina women." He would hastily add, "Judging by my lovely wife, of course!" when I gave him that look—yes, my husband possessed many "idiot-syncracies."

Ever since Auntie Lina introduced Tom to the Filipino delicacies Mama never mastered—lumpia, pansit, adobo, pinakbet, tinola, paksiw, sinanglaw, etc.—Tom would compliment Filipinas with adjectives I would prefer he reserved for food: "delectable," "appetizing," "delicious," "mouth-watering" (this particular one was utilized for infant Josie who peed at him).

"Thomas!" I would declaim, my feminist ire blazing. "Thomas—stop objectifying Filipina women!"

But my husband wouldn't stop the practice until, he said, I would learn to cook Filipino food. I didn't cook. I was proficient in dialing the phone for take-out Chinese. And since Mama never learned how to cook, I saw no reason to change my (lack of a) cooking habit.

In any event, Tom discovered Camille as we explored my grandmother's neighborhood. None of the houses were bordered by fences and we sometimes found ourselves walking across a neighbor's yard. We approached Tata Bino's house to admire his tall mango tree. I saw a stick propped by its trunk and hoped to dislodge a few of the globes I loved to eat with salt or the fish sauce known as baggoong. I knew Tata Bino wouldn't mind as he remembered my passion for green mangos. He had been among the villagers who welcomed us during our first evening in Santo Tomas.

"Hija, you still like those mangos?" he had asked after recalling how he used to feed them to me when I was a child. To my delight, it was mango season and he said I should feel free to avail myself of the fruits within his garden.

I began to show Tom how to dislodge a mango by catching its branch within the carved V tip of the pole, then twisting the pole until the fruit fell. Tom was not as enthused as I was over mangos and quickly became bored. Looking around the yard, he spotted Camille peeking shyly at us from behind Tata Bino's kitchen door.

"Oooooohhhhhh, you yummy little thing. Look at those dark sparkling eyes. And such a pink nose you have," the idiot, I mean, my husband, started crooning at her. "Come over here where I can see you better, you little dumpling."

Camille gave a sound that seemed a cross between a snort and a giggle. Slowly, she approached my husband as he continued to spout off, "That's right you little delectation...come to me, come to me. Why, look at your belly —how nicely your tum-tum curves. I bet you are fed better than my wife feeds me. Come over here, you yummy matzo ball, you scrumptious pot sticker, you mouth-watering bit of salami, you tender teriyaki...."

Susmariosep, I thought and turned to thwack him on the head with the stick. That's when I noticed him cuddling her. "What's your name?" he asked, his face an inch away from hers. Camille's cheeks were pink and covered with a slight fuzz of hair.

"You can name her whatever you want," Tata Bino yelled down to us from his bedroom window over which he had watched the scene unfold. Later, Tom would whisper to me, "That's outrageous. Tata Bino didn't even name her. What kind of a callous attitude is that to a member of his household!?"

Thus, did Tom name her "Camille" because "Camille sounds French and doesn't she also remind you of a Napoleon pastry brimming with cream?" That time, I did thwack Tom across the shoulders with the stick but the name stuck.

❧

Camille, Camille...how my husband loved you! You are forever a part of him...

❧

Since most of the days of our two-week visit were marked by plenty of abundant dinners, Tom's obsession with Filipino food didn't abate. It began with our first evening in Santo Tomas. I wasn't surprised by the feast that awaited us. But, oh, I was moved by the fact that the banquet apparently was a belated wedding celebration. Tom and I already had been married for seven years but my friends and relatives wanted to celebrate with us in person. I ended up sniffling my way throughout the evening as I felt the affection of the residents of my childhood town. In the middle of the dining table was a tiny pedestal highlighting a wedding cake Baroquely festooned with cream ribbons and roses. The wedding album we had prepared years back was displayed on another table so that everyone could go through its pages again.

Tom and I drooled over the plastic-sheathed table brimming with so much food it looked like a lush abstract expressionist painting. Beginning with that first night of our Santo Tomas visit, Tom would turn his wet face towards me after blissfully sweating his way through his dinner and promise, "Eileen, if you don't learn to cook food like this I'll keep objectifying Filipinas with adjectives that will offend your feminist sensibility!"

Idiot, I would think in response as I considered how unappetizing he looked with his sated, dripping face.

❧

Camille, Camille…how my husband loved you! You are forever a part of him…

❧

Tom became particularly enamored with a beauty mark, an inch-wide black mole sprouting a five-inch hair, on the left side of Camille's nose.

"At first I thought it grotesque," Tom said as he twisted the giggling Camille's face this way and that to take a close look at it. "But it actually enhances the loveliness of her complexion, her otherwise pink face. Don't you think?"

This, from someone who once promised he'd never look at another female again after our first date.

"It's a matter of contrast, you know," the fool continued. "Were it not for this mole, this flaw, the delicate rose tinge of Camille's cheeks would not be so obvious. Wasn't it your beloved Baudelaire who once noted the importance of contrast by observing how the sky sighted between two chimneys offers a more profound idea of the infinite than a great panorama seen from a mountaintop?"

Oh puh-leeeeeaaaazzzze, I thought, disgusted. *Now he's quoting a poet!*

Still, I thought it beneath my dignity to display my misgivings over Tom's new obsession. I kept silent, but must have failed occasionally to hide my misery since both my grandmother and Tata Bino were moved on separate occasions to take me aside and advise, "It's just a short innocent infatuation. It'll pass."

I counseled myself that there was no point in doubting whether my husband would cease his obsession; I knew our visit to Santo Tomas was due to end in several days and, thus, managed to remain silent over this latest of Tom's "idiot-syncracies."

❧

Camille, Camille…how my husband loved you! You are forever a part of him…

❧

But I was not a saint. After days of watching Tom spend much of his time accompanied by Camille, I lost control one afternoon. Tata Bino's sister, Nana Adele, invited my parents, Tom and I to a lovely lunch. Nana Adele was a widow who lived by herself in a small lime-green house surrounded by rice fields; reaching her house required a two-hour drive. Tom insisted on taking Camille with us.

Even my saintly mother was provoked enough to hint, "Tom, Camille may not like long jeepney drives."

"As a matter of fact," my mother continued as she turned to Tata Bino, "didn't you say that Camille gets dizzy if she has to be in a vehicle for more than half an hour?"

Unfortunately, Nana Adele was long-renowned for her dinardaraan, which happened to be Tata Bino's favorite dish. Most people cooked this meat dish, redolent with vinegar and spices, by using pork; to Tata Bino's delight, Nana Adele used dogmeat. Thus, did Tata Bino reply, "Well, yes. Camille, indeed, gets quite sick. But not if I'm there to soothe her."

Quickly, Tom leapt at the opening.

"Excellent, excellent!" he said, a grin splitting his sunburnt, peeling face. "You must join us, Tata Bino!"

How did I end up with this tomato? I thought.

They all looked at me. Ooooops: I had uttered my comment out loud. I stalked away rather than apologize. I also reminded myself that only three more days remained before we had to return to New York. *New York—where we obviously could not take Camille with us*, I thought and, thus, reined in my temper.

Just as Santo Tomas had welcomed us with a banquet, they sent us back to New York with another major feast. The afternoon before my family was scheduled to go to Manila and hop on a plane back to the United States, everyone contributed to a marvelous potluck celebration that Tata Bino hosted in his newly cleaned yard.

All of my favorite foods—and those that Tom claimed to be his favorites, a claim that everyone laughingly dismissed because they all learned that Tom would eat, and love, anything—were displayed on three long tables. But the obvious highlight—proffered on a large painted ceramic plate—was a suckling pig. It laid atop layers of banana leaves on a plate centered on the table. Under the tropical sun, it gleamed with a radioactive glow. The *lechon* skin had turned amber from Tata Bino's secret glaze recipe. To memorialize our family's return to the United States, an imported red apple was stuck in the pig's mouth.

"Tom—you must have the first bite of the *lechon!*" Tata Bino proclaimed. It was the first time I saw a crowd of Filipinos become unanimously silent. They also seemed to have deferred breathing as they watched my grinning, red-faced husband shake hands as he sweated his way through the crowd. With clear expectation, Tata Bino awaited him. Not a sound could be heard for miles as people watched Tom approach the middle table. Not a sound could be heard for miles as we witnessed Tom take his first sight of the pig. Not a sound could be heard for miles as we breathlessly observed Tom gulp, then ask in a high-pitched voice, "What's that?"

Dispassionately, I noticed how being roasted for hours didn't eliminate the mole from Camille's cheeks.

"Ahhhh! This is *lechon*! Roasted pig! A prized Filipino delicacy!" Tata Bino enthused. He pretended not to hear Tom gasp when he poked a knife through the pig's crispy side.

Tata Bino twisted the knife and hooked out a piece of pink meat attached to a piece of amber skin. He placed the morsel on a small plate and extended it to Tom.

"As someone who has honored us by enjoying Filipino food, you must have the first bite!"

Not a sound could be heard for miles as Tom looked at the morsel in horror.

"Since you so loved Camille, I thought I must give her to you!" Tata Bino added gleefully.

I let my eyes pass over my beloved friends and relatives. As each felt my stare, each looked back blandly. We all knew: the tiniest piece of a smile, the subtlest wink, the briefest choked-off laugh, would unravel our conspiracy and we would collapse to the ground with robust, eye-watering, belly-clutching, heart attack-inducing laughter. We could never be so rude to the visiting American husband of someone whose family was held in high esteem—a family who just had donated funds to build a fence around the church courtyard.

But having been the tortured—and, worse, pitied—wife for nearly two weeks, I spoke.

"Honey," I said in my most honeyed voice. "Everyone has worked so hard to make this banquet the most memorable you shall ever experience. And now they are honoring you by offering the first bite of Tata Bino's prized *lechon!*"

Tom turned his face towards me. I met the panic in his lovely green eyes with the steel of a *bolo* knife.

He gulped, whispered "Yes, dear," and raised a hand to accept the plate Tata Bino was offering him with an expression of utmost innocence.

Tom gingerly picked up the morsel, closed his eyes, and popped Camille's flesh into his mouth. I noticed that he didn't chew. He simply swallowed quickly. I had never seen him swallow anything so quickly.

The crowd erupted with much applause and toasts for a good life— *Mabuhay*! Grinning so hugely his blackened molars showed, Tata Bino swiftly added another succulent piece onto Tom's plate.

"You like my cooking, hah? Please have another! I can tell you really like my cooking!" Tata Bino proclaimed.

Faced with otherwise insulting Tata Bino, Tom reached again for the morsel, closed his eyes and popped another piece of Camille into his mouth.

I looked around and asked innocently, "Anyone have any tapey? I bet my husband would love to try our potent rice-wine."

Thus, did everyone finally give in to their laughter. The crowd roared and roared as if they had never ever in their entire lives heard anything as funny as my query for tapey. My grandmother shook her head, giggled into her handkerchief, then motioned for one of the men to offer a glass of tapey to Tom.

"As for me," I yelled, quieting the crowd. "Tata Bino—please cut me some choice pieces from that baby. I've wanted to get my hands on Camille for a long, long time…"

❧

Camille, Camille…how my husband loved you! You are forever a part of him…

Homeland

"*M*agandang umaga. Good morning," announced Reverend Nestor, hands raised as he beamed at the congregation from the pulpit. The Sunday mass was mid-way, and Reverend Nestor was about to commence the "Greetings" session.

"I notice several new faces in the congregation today. Would you please introduce yourself or be introduced?"

Mr. and Mrs. Lactan stood up from the front pew and turned to face the congregation.

"We are delighted to introduce the Maldonado family: Peping, his lovely wife, Gloria, and their daughter, Tessie," Mr. Lactan announced, motioning to their seatmates. He spoke slowly, as if to prolong a moment under a spotlight, and his eyes traveled, as if to note who was not paying him sufficient attention. The Maldonados stood up gingerly and turned to offer shy smiles to the congregation.

"I know you all will help me guide the Maldonados in their new life here after they join the membership of our church," said Mr. Lactan. He held court for another five minutes, describing the Maldonado family's lengthy road to California from a fishing town outside Manila.

Two other introductions were made, both of other Filipinos visiting relatives who were members of the church. Over time, with the wave of immigrants from the Philippines, the congregation of the Los Angeles church had become predominantly Filipino or Filipino-American.

I continued to ignore Mama's elbows. Finally, she stood up and announced, "Well, my daughter and her husband need no introduction since most of you were present at this church when they married each other five years ago. But here they are visiting from Chicago, and I would like to present to you again Attorney and Mrs. Wasserstein. This is their first visit back since the wedding."

I tried to ignore Ray's nudges as we both stood. Grinning broadly, Ray insisted on waving to the front, to the back, to the folks sitting in the boxes overlooking the sanctuary. . . to the North, South, East, and West.

"Attorney and Mrs.?" he questioned as we sat down.

"Attorney is an honorific, like doctor, in the Philippines," I whispered back, staring a warning into his eyes. Ray likes to have a good time and is always ready to find humor in all situations.

I turned my attention back to Mama who was patting my hands. I patted hers back.

Seated at the other side of Mama, Papa smiled fondly at me.

"Do you want me to tell the Reverend that journalists also deserve to be addressed by their own honorable titles? Like 'Muckraker Extraordinaire' perhaps?" Ray continued into my ear. I ignored him, deliberately focusing on admiring the interior of my childhood church. I noticed the dust motes dancing on the colorful rays beamed into the sanctuary from the stained-glass windows around the walls. I knew that members of the congregation had baked puto and cakes, hosted folklorico dance fests, and washed cars in the church parking lot for nearly six years to finance the stained glass windows.

Following the mass, the congregation gathered in the church's community room for coffee, assorted home-made snacks and conversation. As we walked through the door, I heard Mrs. Cojuanco's loud, high-pitched voice.

"Did you notice how, as usual, Engineer Lactan made sure his check was face up in the collection box so the rest of us can see how generous he is," Mrs. Cojuanco was informing Lydia, Reverend Nestor's long-suffering wife. I quickly tugged Ray away towards the coffee urns. He would wallow in that conversation.

"He-len, Ra-a-ay," a familiar voice beckoned. Auntie Sheila held out two white napkins topped by yellow slices of cake. "How wonderful to see you both again."

Auntie Sheila felt smaller in my hug than when I last saw her at my wedding. Her smile, however, was still as bright as those I had memorized as the little girl who was her special favorite among our large clan.

"See, I cut you a corner piece because I remember how much you love lemon icing," Auntie Sheila girlishly offered to Ray.

"Sheila, you always know my weak spot," Ray reached for the two-inch square of cake. "And, I must say, you're looking quite fetching. Tell me, how many boyfriends are you juggling nowadays?"

Auntie Sheila's laughter floated up to the ceiling.

"Oh, he is such a lokoloko," she exclaimed to me, patting her hair. Though a widow for ten years, Auntie Sheila had photos of her husband, my Uncle Elmo, in every room of her house.

"That he is," I said, saintly with patience. Ray winked at me as he picked up a white plastic fork from the serving table.

"Well, if it isn't our hope for the Pulitzer Prize someday, eh?" I felt another familiar memory drape itself over my shoulders.

"Mrs. Lactan," I replied with a deliberately visible joy as I turned around within and out of her scratchy, polyester-draped arms.

"You remember Ray," I offered my invincible husband to my former Bible School teacher.

"Of course, of course. How are you Attorney Wasserstein," Mrs. Lactan graciously ignored the icing that Ray left on their handshake.

"We're doing well. Thank you for asking, Lina, isn't it?" Ray prided himself on his memory.

"Ah yes, Lina," Mrs. Lactan repeated. Anyone not looking for it would have missed her slight wince; many Filipinos such as Mrs. Lactan have never become accustomed to being addressed by their first names by younger people.

"Now, Mrs. Lactan," Aunt Sheila jumped in quickly. "Where is that nice Maldonado family? I would like to meet them and welcome them to our church."

"Well, we should present our regards to Reverend Nestor, as well," I said, catching Ray's arm.

"Oh, sure, I see him over there by the window"; occasionally, Ray could be quick. "How very nice to see you again, Mrs. Lactan," we said in unison.

"I'll see you for dinner at the house," Auntie Sheila whispered as she led Mrs. Lactan away towards the Maldonado family.

Reverend Nestor was surrounded by some of the church's notables: Mr. Pascua who oversaw the church's finances, Mrs. Leyte who was in charge of Sunday School for the children, Mr. and Mrs. Saturnino who always ensured there were flowers on the church altar, Mrs. Cruz who was president of the Women's Circle, and Randy Chua who was the counselor for the church's teenagers. We were greeted as long-lost members returning to the congregation's fold.

"Tell me, where do you go to church in Chicago?" Reverend Nestor asked.

"We-e-ll," Ray started, at a loss for once. He looked at me.

I looked at him.

He looked at me.

I gave up.

"Well, we have found a very nice synagogue along Park Lane," I said. Trying for linkage, I added, "Park Lane is not so far from a Filipino community in Chicago. It's where some of Papa's cousins live."

"Oh, how nice, how nice," Randy nervously offered as the others nodded their heads up and down, though looking a bit unsure as to what they were agreeing.

"And it's always good to be close to some family, especially since you are so far away from your Mom and Dad," Mrs. Chua gently added.

"Synagogue—is that Jewish?" Mr. Pascua bluntly asked.

I held my breath as Ray replied, "Yes, indeed, yes. My family is of that faith."

Again, the crowd nodded up and down as they thought a bit.

"Well, well, how interesting," offered Mrs. Saturnino.

I smiled weakly at her. Mr. Pascua, a furrow on his brow, kept staring fixedly at Ray.

"So, then tell us," Mr. Pascua finally asked just before their silence was about to turn me into the fidgeting little girl familiar to most of them, "How does it feel to be one of God's chosen people?"

Mr. Pascua's tone was respectful, almost awed.

God's chosen people. Relief flooded through me. Still, I couldn't bear to listen to how Ray's comedic nature might twist to Mr. Pascua's heart-felt question. I mumbled an excuse and quickly returned to the coffee urns. From across the room, everyone looked fascinated as Ray held forth. And held forth. And held forth. I could see that Ray spoke in all seriousness. Not a single laugh was shared among the crowd that had begun to gather around him.

A half hour later, Ray extricated himself and returned to my side.

"I told them, you know," he said, looking quite pleased with himself.

"Told them what?"

I was concerned that Ray had left such a serious crowd behind him. I hoped he hadn't offended them. When I was a little girl, I was quite shy with people. But as I grew up basking in the love and support of the congregation of my childhood church, I learned to be more outgoing, more confident. I doubt that I would have succeeded as a journalist if I had remained so diffident at interacting with other people. Just last month, an article I'd written about a survivor of Ferdinand Marcos—once, he was in a hole with the barrel of a gun shoved into his mouth while his torturer played Russian roulette—made the front page of *The Chicago Times*.

"Well, think of all that oil! I told them that *my* people should have turned right instead of left when they left Egypt."

As Ray laughed loudly at his own joke, the entire room turned towards him and smiled. Relieved, I grinned back and rolled my eyes upwards as if to say, "What can I do?"

As I basked in the crowd's acceptance, I knew then that though many more years may pass before I next returned to my childhood church, I will never fear introducing any person I will become in the future.

When Nana Died

She was old enough to be my grandmother. She even looked like Nana: wrinkled cheeks, a permanent furrow on her brow, thinning white hair, a slightly stooped back, black polyester pants, an acrylic sweater whose sleeves ended too soon and a smile indicating an eagerness to please. Her hands shook under my glare, pleading and raised defensively as I screamed at the top of my lungs: "Starch! Starch! Starch!"

She had forgotten to starch the collars of my husband's shirts. In the back of the laundry, by a curtain thrust aside when I first started screaming, her son stood as still as a statue except for his eyes which kept twitching between me and his mother. He knew I was attacking the old woman trembling in front of me. But, like his mother, he could not speak English well enough to discuss my problems, let alone calm me down—calm down a most important customer who unfailingly dropped off shirts to be hand-laundered and ironed, six shirts a week, 52 weeks a year for a pricey $3.75 a shirt. He could only stand there, red-faced, a tic pulsing under his left eye and breathing quickly through an open mouth.

As I continued to yell at his mother, my spirit rose and hovered over the scene. I had not seen my shimmering twin sister since I berated my father for once insisting that my husband, a lawyer, advise a distant cousin who had arrived illegally in the United States. There were so many "cousins" arriving as a dictator pillaged our birthland, forcing many of its citizens to leave.

"Immigration is not his specialty," I said truthfully. But when I added, "And I'm sick of these people we barely know trying to cadge free legal services," I felt my ears pop and my spirit float away. My spirit had a habit of leaving my body whenever she thought I was committing a shameful act; she would waft off into the air with, depending on the situation, an expression of sadness, disgust or anger rippling on her translucent face.

As I screamed about the importance of stiff collars on my husband's 100%-cotton shirts, my spirit again departed. Floating above the wall dryers, she pursed her lips and inclined her head at the son—a young teenager with hair cut raggedly across his forehead, a large pimple on the left side of his nose and eyes so wide I could have counted the veins surrounding his pupils. The furrow in the middle of his brow seemed to deepen, as if he was aging visibly in front of my eyes.

I was not a bully. Indeed, I had always considered myself rather nice, polite and especially respectful of people who were of my grandmother's age. But there I was, purple-faced, shaking, hands clenched and on the verge of saying *it* to the elderly Chinese woman. *It*. "Why don't you go back where you came from?"

I stopped my tirade only when, looking away from the boy whose chest began heaving behind his thin t-shirt, my eyes stumbled on a bare patch of pink and seemingly paper-thin skin on the center of his mother's scalp. It made my tongue rear, silenced me abruptly. The patch of flesh reminded me of my grandmother's funeral the previous day. After kissing Nana's forehead as she had laid in her coffin, I had touched her hair. I remembered my disconcertion at feeling how her hair had become so sparse that my fingers could differentiate individual strands against the flesh of her scalp. They had felt like scars.

I turned from the laundry woman's bowed face—her quivering chin—and walked towards the exit. I halted once to say without turning around, "My husband will be back." As I opened the door, I sensed my words hanging in the air as if I had meant them as a threat, which only made me walk faster from their silence.

But I knew as I left the laundry that I would be the one to return. As soon as I could regain self-control, I would return to apologize. My grief at my grandmother's death was not the burden of the Chinese family who I knew worked long hours to meet their rent. I knew they worked hard because we had spoken many times of the burdens of immigration and assimilation in slow, broken English punctuated with smiles and empathetic sighs. We had shared such a conversation just the previous week when I had dropped off the batch of shirts they had forgotten to starch. As for my grandmother, she had been the only person who had managed to soothe her American-born but distinctly Asian-looking granddaughter when I had raged at how the bullies of my childhood made me suffer. The bullies always yelled at me, "Ching. Chong. Chinee. Why don't you go back where you came from?" I was not Chinese but to them, all Asians looked alike.

Halting on a street corner, I sensed my tears attracting attention from the crowds enjoying the unseasonal warmth and cloudless sky of a winter day. But I continued to watch the sidewalk dampen by my feet.

A Ghost Haunting

". . . Exile from the land of one's childhood can sometimes prove the most certain way home. . . . Lost . . . is the tactile immediacy of the past, the physical evidence of experience. Gained is the costly freedom to remember, to turn place and time over and over in the imagination, all the while knowing that no one story can explain the past."
—John Burnham Schwartz

"It couldn't have been easy adjusting to a new country, a new lifestyle. It must have been like walking through a minefield," Jeremy said. His voice was husky, coarsened by sleepless nights. When he looked up, I saw his confusion in the blood-lined, miniscule cracks across his eyes. "Perhaps that's why she tried to recreate herself into someone she thought we'd find more attractive. But she also ended up hiding her true self and here I am, after two years of loving her, asking the bathroom mirror: 'Who was she?'"

As I listened to Jeremy, I thought about how we had never wondered whether we were too hard on her: Marites, a newly-arrived Filipino immigrant when we met her waitressing at the Indigo Club in Greenwich Village. Her heart-shaped face featured a pert nose hovering over reddened lips. A black silk cord flowed over her white t-shirt, ending in a silver cross. Black jeans and high-heeled workmen's boots completed her garb as well as displayed an elegant line to her slim body.

"Oh, the manager is a friend. I'm just helping out until he finds a new waitress," she confided as she distributed our drinks. Flipping back her long wavy hair, she noticed how she caught Jeremy's eye. She bantered with him and, in a gesture I would understand later as to bely her serving tray, happened to mention her interest in attending one of New York's art schools. As the evening progressed and more drinks were served, they flirted with observations about the blues band fronted by a 300-pound lady singer.

"Notice how, on the low notes, the silk shudders apart to showcase the canyon of her cleavage," I overheard Jeremy teasing her.

With a giggle dimpling her cheek, she replied, "She does that on purpose, you know. She once showed me how, with a twitch of her shoulders, she can part the top of her dress to display her bounty.

"'Ho-neeey, ahhhh know what men wants an' ahhhh aim to pleeeazzze.'" Jeremy and Marites laughed into each other's eyes over Marites' imitation of the singer.

Jeremy invited Marites to sit at our table after the club emptied around us. We were mostly investment bankers celebrating newly awarded bonuses. Eagerly, she turned her attention to us, anticipating that another way to Jeremy's heart was through his friends.

"You all work on Wall Street? My goodness—that's so impressive. I just know I would be so lost in the world of high finance. That is so outside my own background," she said, smiling upon us all. Charming, we mostly thought, despite the transparency of flattery that insistently offered an invitation to ask about her own "background." At least one of us retained the politeness to follow through, so that when we finally left the club for eggs at a nearby diner, we already were satiated with detailed accounts from Marites' earlier lifestyle: shopping day-trips to Hong Kong which, she said, were not atypical for the monied elite of Manila; comparisons of Swiss versus Massachusetts boarding schools; an ancestor who was her country's first Minister of Finance; and an uncle whose company once redecorated Malacanang Palace under the directives of Imelda Marcos.

Jeremy, my husband David, and our friends at Wittgenstein & Co., the most profitable investment bank on Wall Street, initially accepted her as one of us. Marites had not needed to attempt to impress. We understood with no particular objection that we were bound to accept her once Jeremy liked her. Jeremy is an amicable enough guy. But within the finance community dominated by Wittgenstein, we were mostly conscious that Jeremy created RESETS, loans with interest rates adjusted every two years to reflect the market. RESETS attract investors who otherwise would sit on their monies as they wait for interest rates to rise. When Jeremy captured hundreds of millions of dollars with his invention, as well as the cover of *Business Week* as Deal-Maker of the Year, he joined the elite whose friendships served to heighten credibility within Wittgenstein's world.

Marites benefited from Jeremy's repute. We overlooked her obvious eagerness to move into Jeremy's Upper East Side apartment. We applauded when she threw away Jeremy's bookshelves of bricks and planks as part of overhauling his aging, dorm-room décor that he'd been too busy to update. Consciously considering ourselves his personal friends and not just business associates, we approvingly thought that Jeremy, finally, was developing beyond the one dimension of his career by committing to a relationship and expensive, Roche BoBois furniture. We gave credit to Marites as the catalyst. No one actually cared for the flowery piece of fluff that Marites draped atop their kitchen window, but she created a pleasant enough home for Jeremy and, initially, we all wished her well for those efforts. Certainly, she was the only woman Jeremy ever dated whose concern for Jeremy rivaled that of Nadja, his mother. Nadja was infamous for hopping on planes with home-made chicken soup every time Jeremy had a cold. She would rush to New York from her ranch in Bakersfield, California where Nadja had brought her Oklahoma oil bounty to retire. When Nadja sniffed at Marites, we considered it a logical reaction and refused to fault Marites.

"Oooohhhh, do you think Nadja disapproves of me?" Marites asked all of us during the early days of her relationship with Jeremy. Sometimes, her eyes still glistened like a black pavement from a recently departed rain. Initially, her question always trailed off into our automatic expressions of support, our jokes and soothing replies easy enough to offer until her countenance brightened once again.

Nevertheless, we were untouched by Marites' lack of involvement in much of our conversations over the dinners she created on Jeremy's behalf. With hindsight, our chatter of Wall Street deals and related gossip must have been incomprehensible to her, with no perceivable entryways through which she could enter into our discussions. In the beginning, we simply displayed our typical insensitivity to those not knowledgeable about the financial matters that monopolized our days. But much later, we became attuned to the diminishment of her stature, even as her embellishments grew more fantastic, more frantic as she must have sensed something slipping from her grasp.

"During my aunt's recent visit to India, she bought the emerald collection of a Maharajah whose descendants fell on hard times," she once volunteered expectantly over the chicken she had barbecued on the grill of their apartment's terrace. As on other occasions, we nodded politely and some of us, for Jeremy's sake, eased the conversation into another topic before others at the table pounced on Marites' latest effort. With a murmured excuse, Marites would leave as we continued our conversations with each other. Only I noticed when she fidgeted with the karaoke equipment in the living room, obviously hoping others might take note. Or perhaps the others did notice, from the corner of their eyes, the glitter-dusted machine but ignored it to spare Jeremy the embarrassment of having us watch him watch Marites mouth along to Barry Manilow tunes in his living room.

Among us, Daphne was the kindest to Marites. Daphne was one of five daughters of a single mother with a wandering attention span. When she was in high school, her family stayed at the Emperor's Palace, a Times Square hotel beset by drug dealers in hallways, rats and roaches in poorly ventilated rooms and frequently stopped plumbing in ancient bathrooms. During pensive breaks in late-night, deal-making sessions at Wittgenstein, Daphne sometimes shared stories of her younger days to the fascination of most Wittgenstein bankers who were reared in the comfort of middle to upper-middle class suburban lives. That she did so with no embarrassment impressed us as much as the obscenely wealthy upbringing of the Trust Fund Babies who also wandered Wittgenstein's corridors.

Unlike others at Wittgenstein as they became more familiar with Marites, Daphne never spoke ill of Marites. But her silence failed to stop others from believing that they knew Daphne's thoughts on Marites. Everyone remembered how Marites rather enthusiastically expressed "Congratulations!" when Daphne introduced a new boyfriend, William, at one of Wittgenstein's summer picnics. In a manner which looked designed for William to overhear, Marites asked Daphne, "Isn't it nice not to come home to an always empty apartment, especially after your long days of work?" Well, loneliness is a bear, but we also thought the boyfriend was picayune.

"A poet?" Jeremy queried with a lift of his eyebrows. "I suppose I could call myself that, too, if I had nothing to do but spend from an inheritance of profitable funeral parlors."

Jeremy merely voiced our thoughts; we are not adept at understanding people who are just passing time. Ultimately, Daphne must have agreed with our assessment of William as their relationship failed to last through a full summer's worth of Long Island beach weekends. After that, Daphne's romantic life was stark, just as it had been for several years before that summer picnic. *Still*, we all thought conveniently, how dare Marites condescend to Daphne, the unanimous favorite within our jaded, cynical crowd.

Mimi, on the other hand, was Daphne's complete opposite. Mimi delighted in torturing the junior bankers who called her "Valkyrie from Hell" because of her mane of red hair, quarterback shoulders and six-foot height.

She once marched into an analyst's office and threw his 20-page research paper into the trash can. "Is it too much for you to figure out the tax implications of one idiotic deal?" she screamed, hands on hips and her face an inch from the analyst's nose. As he shrunk back, the phone rang with their Canadian client looking for the answer to his tax question. Placing the client on the speaker phone, Mimi reached for the analyst's paper among the garbage and read from its conclusion.

"Perfect. Perfect. Exactly what we hoped to hear in order to proceed," waxed the rhapsodic client. After hanging up the phone, Mimi stared at the analyst whose relief was starting to smooth his brow. She deliberately drew out more moments of silence, waiting until the analyst's eyes shrunk back to human size, before resuming her glare and pronouncing: "You're just damn lucky the client is as moronic as you are!" The analyst was dispatched to discover the *true* answer to the tax question, though both understood the impossibility of improving on the answer already provided and already correct. Innumerable junior bankers have left Wittgenstein rather than work for Mimi a second time. Yet we opened our circle to her. As Jeremy once noted wryly, "With her financial acumen, she could be a mass murderer and still be trotted out as one of Wittgenstein's most valued assets."

About Marites, Mimi only scoffed. "Can you imagine," she cackled, her orange fingernails raking the air over an appreciative audience during one lunch in Wittgenstein's executive dining room. "She was so proud of Jeremy, whispering about his million-dollar bonus. I almost revealed mine so she could run back to Jeremy asking why I got more!"

David. My quiet husband, originally from Squirrel Hill, Pittsburgh and the only man known to have better manners than George Bush, Sr., observed Marites. Shook his head, but kept his thoughts from our friends at Wittgenstein where he managed their legal department. Merely once commented to me before jetting off to Washington on another lobbying effort, "Another problem is that you are known within Wittgenstein."

Me. I, a *Pinoy*, Filipino, too. But what the Wittgenstein deal-makers saw in me and compared with Marites is a Filipino-American lawyer practicing at Carignan, Malbec & Verdot, arguably the best corporate finance law firm servicing Wall Street. Ethnic, yes, but sanitized by the trappings of an Ivy League education, a high-rise office surrounded by superb views of Midtown Manhattan and my credenza's graveyard of lucite trophies commemorating service on a portfolio of transactions valued in the billions of dollars. Even Mimi was polite to me. Once, as we shared a dinner of Chinese takeout in one of Wittgenstein's conference rooms, she admired my shoes. To Mimi, shoes were the coincidental avenue for praise. Gracefully, I accepted her compliment, fully aware that the mundanity of footwear did not remind everyone of the excess that decimated a country's future.

I admit resenting the ease with which Jeremy's friends engaged in comparisons, even though all were to Marites' detriment. To me, they chortled about the "allowance" Marites received from Jeremy. No wonder she had a great wardrobe. No wonder she was devoted to him. No wonder she was a happy camper. I saw their thoughts clearly: leering, grimacing, winking, judging. And we all knew (because Marites informed us amid squeals over Jeremy's generosity) that when Jeremy went with Marites to the Philippines last December, he paid for plane tickets and gave her another $1,000 for Christmas, in part to address dental problems because, as Marites said, dentists charge less over there. Undoubtedly true, except I also do not believe that relatives charge each other *over there*. There I go, grimacing at her as well. In truth, I was disturbed that we shared our origins and, thus, comparisons could be thought appropriate.

I was ten years old when I arrived in the United States. Old enough to remember my parents' struggle with our new country. Old enough to recall their hurt at encountering discrimination from grocery clerks who rudely ignored questions to bosses who denied promotions for no defensible reasons. Old enough to remember their confusion at facing taunts from kids—"Go back where you came from! Ching, chong, chinee!"—simply by walking down a street. I should have been sympathetic to Marites' flailing attempts to ingratiate herself with Jeremy's crowd. But I remained aloof. Once, I remarked at a Wittgenstein dinner that, *indeed*, I was from a different part of the Philippines from where Marites was born.

When Jeremy ended his relationship with Marites, it was as if all at Wittgenstein breathed a collective sigh of relief. They rallied and crowded around Jeremy, promoting the rightness of his decision. It was only after Jeremy's decision that I remembered how Marites once asked my advice when we were both caught on the quiet side of a hotel ballroom hosting another Wittgenstein social function. She queried, tentatively, whether she should share the title of her Manila condominium investment with Jeremy. Or maybe a will, she suggested, in case something ever happened to her. I don't remember how I answered. I barely remember the details of the conversation. I only realize now the generosity of her offer which contradicts her image as a gold-digger. I wonder now if there are other facets Marites that we all missed in our eagerness to foster the growing criticism about someone we considered alien. I wonder now if there were other overtures by Marites that I carefully ignored at the time and carefully forgot thereafter.

Marites. The accent thick enough to curl my toes. The lack of weapons with which to compete with careers involving power lunches, offices overlooking clouds, frenzied bouts of negotiations that lasted through the nights and, always, the addictive adrenaline of chasing the next big score. We forgot that, at least initially, she must have made Jeremy happy. Sufficiently happy so that, unknown to his other Wittgenstein friends, Jeremy remains tortured over his decision to leave her. I will never forget Marites' sartorial influence and Jeremy's relish of his new dapper look during the early days of their relationship. His shirts blossomed from plain white into stripes of all width and color, with some dangling cuffs that allowed him to showcase elegant cufflinks of gold loveknots, diamond-edged ebony squares and demure circlets of silver and mother of pearl. And his ties: so tantalizing were the patterns of swords, ribbons, Medieval knights, polo players riding high over speeding horses, Irish tartan, mini coats of arms and gold bullions. Still, all we credited Marites was epitomized in her three-week attempt to be a real estate broker: the first week of excitement at being able to discuss her own career, the second week of bragging about other brokers' successes and making them her own, and the third week of noting the money to be made in commissions notwithstanding none of her own. "Vulgar," sniffed Mimi.

Marites. When I visit Stockton, California, when I am far from Manhattan and in Mama's kitchen eating her adobo, pansit, pinakbet and paksiw, Marites becomes more familiar. With every visit to Stockton, I fend off Papa's questions about how much money I make. With his placid manner, long-receded hairline and belly plumped up through age, he is a smiling Buddha in a white t-shirt as he gently quizzes me at the kitchen table. I fend off those questions, knowing my brothers and sisters, some still living with my parents, are straining from the living room to overhear. Fend off those inquiries because I don't want them to know that my annual income is more than all of theirs combined, more than Mama and Papa made together during their first five years in this country. But, always, I give up and quantify specific amounts—during my last visit, the number grew to $75,000 a year. Sufficiently high for them to reconcile some of their immigrant sacrifices. Not sufficiently high to push it beyond their imaginations. Mimi and others at Wittgenstein do not realize that *Pinoys* commonly talk about people's salaries.

Marites. Since she stopped hovering within the Wittgenstein landscape, I am touched by strange desires to take her side, to defend her to Jeremy's friends. But she became irrelevant so quickly at Wittgenstein. Only Jeremy has trouble forgetting. After their break-up, Jeremy thought it logical to define me, as another Filipino, to be the expert who can explain how life with Marites turned awry. Over bottomless mugs of coffee, there were so many unexplainable things to Jeremy. Among them was the mystery of the Tondo incident during his visit to the Philippines. Personally, I can understand Marites' horror at the brother who gave Jeremy a tour of Tondo when asked where the so-called average person lives. Faced with explaining the existence of Manila's infamous slum, I can understand her anger. Faced with explaining the existence of Smokey Mountain, the garbage heap through which slum residents scavenge their livelihoods, I can understand her shame. The insecurity was barely beneath the surface and, I imagine, an easy enough cause for Marites' past dissemblements.

But, in turn, I wonder if a Filipino like Marites ever can understand my rage that the "average" Filipino may live in a slum. My rage. It is a rage that erupts without warning in the most unlikely of settings. It is a rage that erupts in the midst of a succulent dinner, the midst of lovemaking, the midst of a wedding, the midst of enjoying a lazy autumn Sunday—a rage that erupts unexpectedly in the midst of blessings. Sometimes, I wish not to feel it simmering within me. Most of the time, I do not begrudge its presence. The rage also makes me feel bigger than I suspect I am. Unlike Marites, I departed from the Philippines before Martial Law was imposed.

Thus, my memory is one of optimism. I remember a period of time when many anticipated the Philippines becoming the booming Japan of the Eighties, a superpower able to provide home-grown opportunities for its people—not a country whose most able minds are often forced to work as manual laborers overseas, and be grateful for the chance to do so. The optimism in my memory is a taste of rust, jarring against what I observed the country had become. The optimism is an ache that will not go away. It is a ghost haunting.

Marites. I know of her as I would a distant cousin. I am an onlooker to her view of the world. When one lives through a dictatorship, daily sufferings and the cessation of hope may cease to become abnormal. How can she be faulted for not understanding the implications of Martial Law, I speculated, when she is a product of that environment? During conversations when we were first becoming acquainted, it was logical that we spoke about our country of origin. Some discussions became political, but I never saw her display awareness of the lost potential for the Philippines had there been the moral political leadership to guide the country's development. But of the Filipino life, I have different memories and the Philippines' lost potential is as real to me as the loving relatives I left behind.

I grew up in a big house, personally designed by my father, on top of a mountain in the city of Baguio. Baguio, whose elevation above the seas create a weather of cool breezes, enrapturing the country's tropical residents to hail the city as a mini-Switzerland, the Summer Capital. Our house was surrounded by spectacular vistas and scenery only rarely interrupted by other houses. Then, the pine trees ruled. Papa hired some men to pour a cement road from the base of the mountain to our front yard. Every holiday season, children in the neighborhood walked up the road to gaze at our Christmas tree. I loved walking up to the house my Papa created with the rewards of his honest entrepreneurship, my head tilted up to the clouds as I pretended the cement road to be a red-carpet runner described in my story books. And once I arrived at the peak, I would spend endless time stretching my gaze over valleys and imagined possibilities beyond other peaks. The cement road was the first in our neighborhood, a bright symbol of modernization. Whenever I think of Papa today, I clearly see the man with the bold gaze, standing self-assuredly on strong legs in his front yard overlooking the rest of the world.

As for *Pinoys* in America, what I know is, mostly, unease.

Unease: a doctor over there, a nurse's aide here; a college professor over there, a secretary here; a farmer over there, an airport janitor here; a pillar of society over there, a member of the peanut gallery here. As for me, unbeknownst to my friends at Wittgenstein, I am accosted sometimes at airports, elevators, restaurants and other public spaces by strangers who consider me familiar because of a memory lingering from some previous stay in the Philippines where they met women eager to attract Americans. They say I remind them of Vangie, Susan, Josefina, Lillian, Emma, and even "Baby" with whom they had quite a rollicking good time. What I always want to say is how totally sure I am that Vangie, Susan, Josefina, Lillian, Emma and, yes, even Baby undoubtedly sought their company solely because of their manly charm—and not because some old parent otherwise would die of starvation back in a village, not because some infant is desperately waiting for milk, and certainly not because there is no alternative for earning daily bread when male relatives are known to have prices on their head for fighting back against the thuggery of a corrupt politician's private army. But I never say anything because they may not understand my brand of sarcasm. I only walk away, marveling at how I once thought that an expensive business suit is like armor.

Yes, armor. Ever since Ferdinand Marcos mugged nearly two decades of progress from the Philippines, I have believed I needed armor against the embarrassment of being defined by the antics of Ferdinand's greed, Imelda's extravagances, the conspiracy of a minority grabbing scraps from the Marcoses' table, and the resulting impoverishment—psychological as well as financial—of many "average" Filipinos.

Ferdinand Marcos. Even as he watched during the waning days of his regime the masses of Filipinos shoving themselves in front of his military tanks, forcing their hearts in front of his military's guns, he could not understand. Even when his own military, ill-equipped to battle the tears and Sampaguita blossoms being shed on their M-16s and Browning Automatic Rifles, broke ranks and joined the people's revolution led by a housewife, Ferdinand Marcos could not understand. But, truly, he had the support of the people, as he claimed in "60 Minutes." After all, he won the presidential election, Ferdinand Marcos announced, ignoring documented accounts of ballot-rigging and murderous intimidation of election overseers. But the image of his swollen face was quickly supplanted. In February 1986, the world's television cameras roamed Epifanio de los Santos and other avenues of Manila, capturing the solidarity of the protesting socialites, slum-dwellers, nuns, prostitutes, businessmen, politicians, urbanites and farmers. For a moment in time, the Filipinos forgot their internal discord and looked larger than life under the spotlight of a hot sun.

I once asked Marites about life during Martial Law. Her family was sufficiently wealthy to live within Manila's prestigious walled suburbs, to send her to Europe as a student, and to gift her with a bounty in jewels to lose in a restaurant venture in Brooklyn. "Oh, I didn't notice much. All we cared about was making a lot of money," she said honestly.

At my silence, she added, "But my father was good to his employees. He funded scholarships for some of the employees' children who wanted to attend college but were otherwise too poor."

At my continued silence, she went on, "We were not different from others, you know. We only wanted to make sure our livelihood survived. I think most people would not have acted so differently in our shoes."

I did not disagree with her then. I do not disagree with her now. I believe most people do not act the rebel, the martyr, the political saviour. I believe most people merely wish to survive, their families to have a decent livelihood and to enjoy a comfortable existence.

❧

Like Wittgenstein's investment bankers, I often work late into the following day's dawn. In my corner of Carignan, Malbec & Verdot's skyscraper, when Manhattan is both dark and sparkling with gems of light beyond my window, I find myself watching my reflection on the glass as I huddle in my leather chair. The shame I feel has never become familiar in order to dilute its burden. Outlined by the lights of the Big City, I see the faces of those who escaped from the Marcos Dictatorship years ago and landed in New York City—their faces haunt me. They mock me. They chastise me. They feel sorry for me. Once, they tried to recruit me to their cause as they picketed in front of the United Nations, in front of the Philippines' embassy on Fifth Avenue, in front of *The New York Times'* offices as its editors interviewed the visiting Marcoses. But I sniffed at them and said their cause was hopeless, that the Filipino was too passive to rebel against Ferdinand and Imelda's conjugal dictatorship.

Then a man insisted, "The Filipino is worth dying for," and offered his own death as proof. An ocean away, my eyes locked on and forever memorized the image of Benigno "Ninoy" Aquino bleeding on the tarmac of Manila airport. Then the Filipino people wore yellow and marched down the boulevards of Manila, eliminating forever the armor I had sought against being identified as a Filipino.

In my younger days, my brothers, sisters, cousins and I spent many evenings at the house of *Apong*, our grandmother. We would fall asleep on bamboo mats spread out in a large room centered on the second floor of her house. We would fall asleep to her bedtime stories of skinny ghosts who love to tickle mischievous children, old men with white beards falling to their knees who look for children who stray from their parents and plump women with restless fingers who love to pinch the cheeks of children who eat too much. Then there was her last benediction for the evening which often had nothing to do with the benign warning of the tale just ended. Individual sticks are easily broken, *Apong* always counseled. But when bundled together, a different matter.

Marites. I now understand that I hear her plea for help only when it is too late. Her face joins those of others haunting the night outside my window until I am forced to close my eyes against the New York City skyline—against its dancing, dazzling lights.

On Imitating A Rhinoceros

I snorted.

Ever since my boyfriend Tom showed me how to make that snorting sound for repelling rhinos—which he learned from a tracking guide in Nepal as a mountain-sized rhinoceros stamped the ground a mere ten feet away—I've welcomed any opportunity to amuse myself by exploding my nose.

That morning, I noisily dilated my nostrils towards my computer screen. I'm a freelance writer always pitching ideas for articles to a wide variety of online and print publications. Thus, I'm often checking emails even though the frequent rejections would reduce me to a blob of Scyphozoa out of water were my skin not as thick as a, well, a rhino.

"You sound like a dying seal," my father lowered his newspaper to opine. He was resting on the horrendous armchair he brought along with him when he moved in with me three months ago. Duct-tape failed to prevent innards of old, yellow foam from sprouting between cracks in the faded brown leather—this glorious object effectively introduced an aesthetic layer of vomit to my attempted post-modern décor in black and white.

"Rhino, Papa. Not seal," I said as I turned towards him. Once again, I considered how much he'd thinned, as well as how his face had come to resemble his chair with its wrinkles and hair inappropriately tufting out from his nose and ears. "Besides, how do you know the sound of a seal in its death throes?"

"YouTube," he said. "What are you baying about?"

Baying? I mentally filed the thought that perhaps Tom was being diplomatic whenever he praised my attempts to repel a rhino as if its dirt-flecked, kayumangi body was on the other side of a flimsy glass window to my floor-level apartment. Right then, I wanted to address my father since he rarely spoke. When awake, he spent much of his time peering at old copies of the now defunct *Filipino-American Post*, often rereading them so that much of their ink was permanently transferred to the tips of his trembling fingers.

"I just got this email from *Who's Who of West Coast U.S.-Americans*," I replied. "They asked if I wanted to be listed in their next volume."

To my surprise, my father slowly set his newspaper on the side table and leaned forward to give me his full attention.

"But that's wonderful, hija," he said, his eyes gleaming. Surprised, I thought, *Is he about to cry?*

"Oh, not really Papa," I said. "It's just a vanity project..."

I was about to explain that *Who's Who* lacks rigor in its selection process and maximizes the number of included people so as to increase the number of people who might order the volume. But my father derailed my thoughts by standing. Once again, I noticed how his right leg trembled.

"Where's that box of my things? I want to show you something."

"In the hallway closet, Papa." I said. "I put it there until you had time to unpack them into your bedroom."

"All I have is time. Time to remember," I heard him say as he shuffled to the hall. I noticed the stoop on his back—it seemed more pronounced than even just yesterday. *I wish you had the strength of a, well, a rhino,* I thought.

I decided to google *Who's Who* while waiting for him to return. I wasn't surprised to learn of "The *Who's Who* Scam" through which respondents' contact information was harvested for phishing. One victim, a Sally Martin of Chicago, said her credit card data was stolen for ordering thousands of dollars worth of plumbing parts that went to a stranger in Philadelphia. Sally said she could trace the theft to *Who's Who* because she'd given them a brand new credit card and only used it that one time before the fraud occurred.

As I heard my father return, I turned to him, saying, "Apparently, there's this Sally..."

I paused as he approached me haltingly, eyes not just gleaming but wet like his wrinkled, spotted cheeks. He held out a book covered in dark-brown material with faded gilt lettering.

I stood and guided him back to his ugly but beloved armchair. As he sat back, I knelt by his side, struck by how his arm felt like naked bone.

"What's this book, Papa?" I softly asked as he held it towards me. But I could see the title from the faded gilt letters:

WHO'S WHO IN AMERICAN YOUTH

"You never got to know Roy, your older brother," Papa said. "He's on page 581."

I took the heavy book and opened it to the page whose page number he'd memorized. The book opened easily to it as the spine had cracked along the page that had been read frequently. There, I saw the name of my brother who had died prematurely in a car accident. I was four years old.

"Your mom—bless her heart and may she be resting in peace—and I received the letter notifying us of Roy's eligibility to appear in this prestigious volume. We assumed it's because he had straight As in high school."

"Wow," was all I could think to say as my finger trailed across my brother's name and the inch-long, small print depiction of his biography. Roy, the young scholar, had enjoyed studying astronomy, history, and José Garcia Villa's poetry. He'd also excelled at basketball, playing forward for his school's varsity team.

My father raised his hand—I could see pale blue veins through his almost translucent skin. I felt again the ground shift as it did the first time I realized much of humanity will learn orphanhood before they die. With a trembling finger, Papa wiped both cheeks.

"We all had arrived in this country just a year earlier from this notice. But it was enough time to have Roy spend his last high school year in an American school. He was a brand-new immigrant but he had undeniable talent."

I was a writer. I spew out words for a living. But, again, all I could think to say was a whispered "Wow..."

"It was an expensive book. But, look—that title must be printed in gold," Papa said as he pointed at the book. "I remember that its price was about the same as an overtime shift I put in at my cousin's gardening company."

I didn't bother sharing that the book was still expensive today—over a hundred dollars per volume despite the fakeness of the leather binding and the lack of real gold forming its title.

"Roy was so young when the accident took him away from us," Papa continued. "But through the years, your Mom and I were comforted by how he did not have a wasted life—he managed to appear in this impressive book!"

"Yes, he did, Papa!" I said as I gently shut the book and gave it back to him. "He was an outstanding scholar-athlete. If you and Mom sacrificed for your children, Roy was worthy."

Papa nodded as he shut his eyes. I saw one hand cradle the book while the other stroked it. The hands relaxed only when he fell asleep. More and more, Papa was either napping or sleeping. The thin skin of his eyelids covered eyes that I knew had seen more anguish than I might ever know. A dictatorship, martial law, torture, and then the furtive flight from a beloved homeland were elements I knew only as stories rather than lived experiences.

When I returned to my computer, I saw Sally Martin's story still on my screen. I closed its link and returned to the rest of my emails—their voluminous existence testified to my attempts not to waste my life. As I reread the email from *Who's Who*, my eyes traveled downward to snag on the sight of my middle-age belly jutting out over my jeans.

I sat back and contemplated *Who's Who*'s email. I didn't bother imitating a snorting rhino as I wondered if I should participate—surely Papa would be pleased to hold a new volume bound in fake leather and caress its fake gold letters. I wondered if my unexpected consideration of *Who's Who*'s offer, scam or not, might stem from a not-new fear of never being able to validate my parents' sacrifices—both had suffered to give me a chance at a better life than one under the tyranny of corruption and poverty.

Then I wondered if my reluctance also might be from lacking faith my father would live long enough to see the book.

Ach! I thought as I tried to hold back a too-familiar feeling of despondence. *If only my skin really was as thick as a rhino's.*

I looked again at *Who's Who*'s invitation to join the ranks of "important people worth knowing." Tenderly, I placed my fingers on the keyboard to respond.

Poetry's Coda

Witnessed in the Convex Mirror: PAGPAG

"Turns dully away. Clouds
in the puddle stir up into sawtoothed fragments"

[half-eaten corncob   *[bone with marrow still untouched*

[fragmented chicken skin   *[an unknown animal's liver*

[the corner of a banana   *[stray rice kernels*

[a fish eye   *[a fish cheek*

[something unidentifiable   *[something one does not want to see*

[a fish tail   *[a fish bone*

[something sweet   *[more sour*

[some more   *[some less*

"Pagpag"—from Tagalog, "to shake off dust or dirt"

All are dropped
twice
into boiling water

Isa, hold breath. Dalawa, hold breath
One, hold breath. Two, hold breath

Do not breathe

The first cleanse washes away the dust or dirt. Result: gray water

The second cleanse, if the hungry get lucky, results in clear water
If not,   ignore
                                                   "walang pera" for another
                                                   cleanse

Heat up everything in one large pot: a stew scaffolded together
by salt
                                      with crushed garlic if one is
                                      lucky
                                      no one ever gets lucky
                                      "walang pera"
                                      only salt

Descend to speechlessness to eat. Descend to speechlessness
as one is eaten

How to choose between   malnutrition versus Hepatitis A
                                             malnutrition versus typhoid
                                             malnutrition versus diarrhea
                                             malnutrition versus cholera

My people—there exists a beautiful word from the Japanese: *kintsukuroi*
the art of repairing with gold so the broken artifact becomes more
beautiful for having been broken

My people—we must eat, even the cuisine of an unknown word
that means "the opposite of *kintsukuroi*"

Sung between each bite:
"walang pera"
              "walang pera"
                            "walang pera"
                                          "walang pera"
                                                        "wal
ang pera"

My people, let us sing.

Never mind the prayer for *saying grace*
"walang pera"

My people, let us sing.

ACKNOWLEDGMENTS

Much gratitude to the editors and publishers of these journals and books where individual stories previously appeared:

Short Stories
"Negros"
>*Bamboo Ridge*, Spring 1996, Editors Darrell Lum and Eric Chock
>*Mobius, The Journal of Social Change*, Fall 1996
>*Contemporary Fiction by Filipinos in America*, Editor Cecilia Brainard (Anvil Publishing, 1997)

"Tapey"
>*Bamboo Ridge*, 2000, Editors Darrell Lum and Eric Chock
>Read by Honolulu Theater for Youth actor, Bulldog, for *ALOHA SHORTS*, August 14, 2005, Hawaii Public Radio, Honolulu, Hawai'i

"My City of Baguio"
>*dis*Orient*, 1997
>*Otoliths*, 2006, Editor Mark Young
>*THE THORN ROSARY: Selected Prose Poems and New (1998—2010)* (Marsh Hawk Press, 2010)
>*Positively Filipino*, 2020, Editor Gemma Nemenzo

"The Man in a White Suit"
>*L'OUVERTURE*, Summer 1997

"Force Majeure"
>*STORYBOARD*, 1999
>*Bamboo Ridge*, Editors Darrell Lum and Eric Chock

"Redeeming Memory"
>*Bamboo Ridge*, 1998, Editors Darrell Lum and Eric Chock

"Pork"
>*Bamboo Ridge*, Editors Darrell Lum and Eric Chock
>*Writing Home*, Editor Ruel S. De Vera (Anvil Publishing, 2002)
>*OurOwnVoice*, 2012, Editor Reme Grefalda

"Homeland"
>*Robin's Nest* (under Pearl Yasmin)
>*Philippine Graphic*, 2000

"When Nana Died"
>*ENCOUNTERS: People of Asian Descent in the Americas*, Editor Roshni Rustomji-Kerns with Rajini Srikanth and Leny Mendoza Strobel (Rowman & Littlefield Publishers, 1999)

"A Ghost Haunting"
>*Moonrabbit Review*, Spring 1995

"On Imitating A Rhinoceros"
Unlikely Stories Mark V, Editor Jonathan Penton

Poems
"ALAALA: A Balikbayan Box for the Residents of Malacanang Palace"
Rigorous, 2019, Editors Rosalyn Spencer and Kenning JP Garcia

"When I Was"
The Bellingham Review, May 2019
NO TENDER FENCES: An Anthology of Immigrant & First Generation American Poetry, Editors Carla Sofia Ferreira, Kim Sousa, & Marina Carreira (fundraising anthology for RAICES, 2019)

"Witnessed in the Convex Mirror: PAGPAG"
Talisman 57, 2019, Editor Ed Foster
Witness in the Convex Mirror (TinFish Press, 2019), Editor Susan M. Schultz

"Witnessed in the Convex Mirror: PAGPAG" begins with a line from John Ashbery's poem, "Self-Portrait in a Convex Mirror."

The author also thanks the Virginia Center for the Creative Arts for a resident fellowship that helped her write portions of this collection, as well as the following writers and their works for helping to inspire portions and/or tenor of these tales: *WORTH DYING FOR*, a biography of Benigno S. Aquino by Lewis Simon (William Morrow & Co.,1987); Milan Kundera's Postscript to his novel, *LIFE IS ELSEWHERE* (Faber and Faber Limited, 1986); novels by Jonathan Carroll and John Burnham Schwartz whose titles have slipped from my memory; *PLANET WAVES*, a novel by Eric Gamalinda (New Day Publishers, 1989); "OUR ISLAND" a poem by Fatima Lim-Wilson (*CROSSING THE SNOW BRIDGE*, Ohio State University Press, 1995); "Poem No. 37" by José Garcia Villa (*SELECTED POEMS AND NEW*, McDowell, Obolensky, New York, 1958 and Bookmark, Inc., Manila, 1993); "IDENTIFICATIONS," a short story by Clinton Palanca (*catfish arriving in little schools*, Editor Ricardo M. de Ungria, Anvil Publishing, 1996); and a poem by Tan Lin whose identity has slipped from my memory but is in his book (*LOTION BULLWHIP GIRAFFE*, Sun & Moon Press, 1996).

As well, I thank Bino A. Realuyo, Lily Mendoza, Veronica Montes, and Jean Vengua for their suggestions and/or advance words or blurbs in support of this book. Salamat as well to Rea Lynn de Guzman for permission to feature her painting "Self-contained" on the book's front cover. I'm also, as ever, grateful to Aileen Cassinetto and Sophia Ibardaloza of Paloma Press for *eagerly* publishing this collection.

Last but not least, the author thanks the Philippine Literary Arts Council who welcomed me warmly in Manila on Nov. 8, 1996 and other Philippine writers who had responded with generosity to my writings and explorations of our shared history, especially Alfred "Krip" Yuson.

ABOUT THE AUTHOR

Eileen R. Tabios has released about 60 collections of poetry, fiction, essays, and experimental biographies from publishers in ten countries and cyberspace. *PAGPAG: The Dictator's Aftermath in the Diaspora* is her third fiction collection. She also recently finished her first long-form novel, *DoveLion*. Her wide-ranging body of work includes invention of the hay(na)ku, a 21st century diasporic poetic form (whose 15-year anniversary in 2018 was celebrated in the U.S. with exhibitions, a new anthology, and readings at the San Francisco and St. Helena Public Libraries) as well as a first poetry book, *Beyond Life Sentences*, which received the Philippines' National Book Award for Poetry. Translated into ten languages, she has edited, co-edited or conceptualized 15 anthologies of poetry, fiction and essays. Her writing and editing works have received recognition through awards, grants and residencies. More information is available at http://eileenrtabios.com

Established in 2016, **PALOMA PRESS** is a San Francisco Bay Area-based independent literary press publishing poetry, prose, and limited edition books. Paloma Press believes in the power of the literary arts, how it can create empathy, bridge divides, change the world. To this end, Paloma has released fundraising chapbooks such as *MARAWI*, in support of relief efforts in the Southern Philippines; and *AFTER IRMA AFTER HARVEY*, in support of hurricane-displaced animals in Texas, Florida and Puerto Rico. As part of the San Francisco Litquake Festival, Paloma proudly curated the wildly successful literary reading, "THREE SHEETS TO THE WIND," and raised money for the Napa Valley Community Disaster Relief Fund. In 2018, the fundraising anthology, *HUMANITY*, was released in support of UNICEF's Emergency Relief campaigns on the borders of the United States and in Syria. palomapress.net